M. L

HAWKEYE
••• HITS THE •••
JACKPOT

HAWKEYE
••• HITS THE •••
JACKPOT

Veronica Heley

Scripture Union
130 City Road, London EC1V 2NJ.

By the same author
Swift Books
Genius at Work
Sky High

Leopard Books
Free-wheeling
Hawkeye of Paradise Row
The Paradise Row Gang

Tiger Books
Good for Kate!

For 6–8s
Natasha's Badge
Natasha's Swing
Natasha the Brownie

© Veronica Heley 1990
First published 1990

ISBN 0 86201 660 6

Phototypeset by Input Typesetting Ltd, London
Printed and bound in Great Britain by Cox and Wyman Ltd, Reading

1

Kate Webb glanced at her letter and screeched, 'Oh, I don't believe it! I just don't believe it!'

Toby and Nikki watched her, toast and margarine suspended in the air. Kate's twins were accustomed to their mother going over the top, but this was something special, even for her.

'What . . . ?' said Nikki, who was always more inclined to rush into danger than Toby.

'Two months notice, that's what! Clear out, find somewhere else to live, and good riddance!'

'What? Why?' said Toby and Nikki together.

'I took a short lease on this maisonette because it was all I could get, and anyway I wasn't sure I'd like living over a shop. Well, I applied for a renewal of the lease some time ago and Jeff said there shouldn't be any problem, because the developers weren't planning to start on this street yet, but that's exactly what they're going to do! Here's the letter from the company. We've to be out by the end of May, two months off.'

Toby put down his toast. He didn't feel hungry any more.

Nikki said, 'But I like it here.'

So did Toby.

'It's all right I suppose, if you don't mind living next to a building site,' said their mum, beginning to recover from the shock, and to make plans. She narrowed her eyes, ruffling her short, dark hair. 'I've got meetings all day, but I'll make time somehow to go down to the Town Hall, see what else they can come up with by way of accommodation. If we're made homeless, then we're entitled to council accommodation of some kind.'

'You mean we might have to move to the flats?' Nikki was horrified. The neighbourhood was dominated by a block of flats that looked like a beached whale, which had been put up at the time when everyone thought high rise buildings were the answer to the housing problem. But they weren't. Or not this lot, anyway. Their street was called Paradise Row, but there wasn't much paradise to be seen.

Nikki was making choking noises, stifling tears. Their mum turned her head away, pretending not to see. Toby thumped Nikki on the back, and said they'd be late for school.

'I don't care,' shouted Nikki. Then she remembered it was swimming that day and she liked swimming, so she stomped off to get her things together.

Toby felt wrenched apart inside, but he couldn't say so. He looked at his mother's averted face, and knew she was feeling it, too. Kate had worked hard to bring them up properly, since their father's death when the twins were young. Her present job, as Youth and Community Worker for this part of the borough, was the best she'd ever had, and this flat was the best they'd ever had, too.

'I'm sorry, Mum,' he said.

'Oh, it'll be all right, I suppose,' she said, throwing up her head, but still not looking at him. 'I shouldn't have relied on Jeff. The doc warned me. He said the whole block was going to have to come down. He's getting out just in time, isn't he? He did say he'd pop in to see us before he moved to his new health centre, but I suppose he's been too busy, as usual.'

Toby saw his mum was trying not to cry, and he looked away. He wasn't called 'Hawkeye' for nothing. He was the one to spot small objects which had fallen on the floor and got lost in the pattern, and he was always the first one to notice changes in the neighbourhood. Sometimes this ability to see things got him into exciting adventures, but today the trouble was all inside the flat, and that wasn't exciting at all.

He looked out of the window, and saw a furniture van arrive. And yes, there was their friend, the doc, in a boiler suit, energetically helping the removal men. The ground floor lock-up beneath the Webb's flat had been the doc's surgery for many years but his practice had outgrown it. The doc was only moving a couple of streets away, but they'd miss him a lot.

The doc looked up and waved to Toby, making signs that he'd see him in a minute.

Toby couldn't bear to talk to anyone, not even the doc, who was one of his best friends. He had to be alone for a while, or he might get to feeling as bad as Nikki and his mum. He grabbed his school case and ran down the stairs. With a bit of luck he'd be too early for any of his friends, and have the walk to school by himself.

The doc shouted after him, but Toby pretended not to hear. It was a nasty misty morning. Or perhaps he needed glasses.

He walked close to the hoardings that surrounded the building site next door. A large church had once stood there, but it had been bombed during the war, and the local children had taken over the waste ground where the nave had once stood, for a playground. The Wasteland, as they had come to call it, had been the scene of many happy hours and two great adventures for Toby and his friends.* The tower, which was all that still

*Described in *Hawkeye of Paradise Row* and *The Paradise Row Gang*.

7

stood of the original building, had become a focus for their quest for something to make sense of life. The doc had helped them with talks in which they had learned the good news about Jesus, and how important it was in everyday life to be part of his church.

Toby had been thrilled when he heard that the church site was to be redeveloped. The tower was to be renovated, and with a smaller nave was to be their own new neighbourhood church. A community centre would be built on the centre of the site, and the end nearest the shops would be given over to public use, for a garden and playground.

But now the builders had arrived to work on the site, there was no peace for anybody within earshot. The roar of diesel engines vied with the traffic. A crane squeaked overhead, and a length of metal pipe was dropped with a deafening clang. The church tower, which had been Toby's refuge from the world, was now unapproachable, encased in a web of scaffolding.

The Wasteland was slowly disappearing as bulldozers and mechanical diggers scooped up soil and rubble and spat it out into a constantly moving line of lorries. The plans for the new, smaller church and adjoining community complex were displayed on one of the hoardings that surrounded the site.

But Toby wouldn't be next door to see the plans brought to life.

'Hi!' Someone hit him on the shoulder. 'I yelled, but you didn't hear me. Got cloth ears, or something?'

It was Toby's best friend, Fats, larger and blacker than ever. Grinning. Toby hated cheerful people today.

'We've got to move,' he said. 'Developers have given us notice. Two months. Mum threw a wobbly, and Nikki's gone off to have a cry.'

'You should be glad to get out of that dump.'

'It's not a dump!'

'You said it was a dump when you first came.'

'That was then. I like it now. Our flat's all right.'

'What, living over a grotty shop, in a terrace that's only just discovered bathrooms? Should have been pulled down yonks ago.'

'For what? To build more flats like yours?'

'Point taken. OK, but with your mum working for the council, they're bound to find her something else. They think a lot of her. Everyone says they've never had a Youth and Community Worker who gets so much done.'

'They never had one before,' said Toby. He had to admit, his mum really was something else. The way she stirred things up, no-one could ignore her.

The two boys waited for a gap in the traffic to cross the road. Another removal van drew up to the kerb opposite, and a big-bellied slovenly-looking man got out and took the padlock off the door of a shop that had been vacant for ages.

'Look!' said Toby.

'Where?' said Fats, and then nodded, seeing what his friend meant. 'More changes. Someone said it was to be a chippie, but me mum said it was going to be a Den of Thieves.'

'A what?'

'Den of Thieves. Pit of Iniquity. You know how me mum talks. Amusement arcade to you. One-armed bandits, electronic games, flashing lights, loud music. You know. Skin you as soon as look at you, me mum says, and she's forbidden us to go anywhere near. I suppose your mum will tell you the same.'

Toby sighed. 'She won't have much time to tell us anything, what with opening the new drop-in centre down the road, and now having to move.'

'Don't take it so bad,' said Fats. 'One flat's much the same as another.'

'Your flats may be all alike, but ours is different. Ours has got two floors, just like a house, and all our rooms are different shapes, and I've got . . .' He swallowed a bit of dirt that had got into his throat from the building site. 'Well, you know. My room is sort of special.'

'Yeah, I know.'

Fats did know, because he spent a lot of time in Toby's room at the top of the house, looking first out of one window onto the street, and then out of the other, the very special window that overlooked the Wasteland and the church tower. The ceiling of Toby's room came right down to the floor at one side, but the sun was in his room almost all day.

Well, not that day, of course. The mist was turning nasty. The noise on the building site wound up a tone, sounding thinner and somehow sinister. The cold fingers of the mist chilled their faces, got into their ears and down their necks.

'Race you!' cried Fats, and pounded off down the road, hands in pockets, school bag swinging.

'Yes,' said Toby, but he didn't try to compete. He turned back, looking to see if Nikki were in sight. He was worried about her. But she was walking along behind with her friend Jan, with Red hopping around the two of them. She was talking nineteen to the dozen, probably telling them all about the move. She'd be all right.

Toby said to himself, Well, I'll be all right too. It's not the end of the world. It just feels like it, that's all.

He tried to concentrate at school, but it was hard going. The others – Red, Skinny and the rest – thought he was stupid to care about leaving the maisonette above the shops. They nearly all lived in the big block of flats that dominated the neighbourhood. Most of the time they moaned about how terrible they were, but now they speculated about who'd died or moved away, to let the Webbs move in. It stood to reason that Kate would have a good chance of getting a council flat for her family.

Toby knew some of the flats were all right, really. It was just that he didn't like flats, much. And nowhere was he going to find another place to live which overlooked the Wasteland and the church, and had so much sun and sky.

On the way home Fats walked with Toby, trying to cheer him up.

'At least it's stopped raining. Should be good for football this weekend.'

Toby grunted. He wasn't into football. The Camera Club was more his scene.

'They're forming a new All-Black football team,' said Fats. 'They want me to join. What do you think?'

Toby shrugged. The idea of Fats going off to join such a team dismayed him. It wasn't that he thought it was a bad idea in itself, but it would mean Fats had less time to be with Toby. Yet how could Toby say, 'Don't: I need you'?

So he shrugged.

Fats frowned, and swung his bag in a giant circle around himself. 'Sounds all right, this team. They've got the gear and all. Proper coaching. But the bottom line is they want a commitment. Three nights a week minimum.'

Toby stopped walking for a moment, and then nodded, and walked on. He told himself he mustn't be jealous of Fats going off with other people.

'They're only taking the best,' said Fats, 'and I'll be on trial for a while. They said we blacks should take a pride in doing things well, show the whiteys, show the world. They go on about all that too much, but I suppose they're right. Only, you and I had plans to do some photography in the City this spring, didn't we? I'd like to do that, too, but . . . I don't see how I can do both, not properly, not with the homework and all. How do you feel about it?'

'All right,' said Toby. What could he say? He couldn't spoil Fats' chance of getting into a good team. Fats was brilliant at football.

They came to the crossroads opposite the church. The flats towered over everything, dwarfing the shabby terraced houses around. Most of the houses had had their ground floors converted to shops ages ago. The furniture van was gone from outside the surgery, and someone had covered the windows inside with white paint.

'Wait for us!' Red came running up, dragging his school bag along the pavement. Skinny followed.

'Is it open?'

They weren't looking at the surgery, or at the building site, but at the newly-opened amusement arcade. Someone had tacked a banner over the door, saying DEN OF DELIGHTS. Underneath it said, Grand Opening – Five Free Tokens each on the first day!

'Brill!' said Red, diving through the open door into the dusky interior. Somewhere inside there were at least two pop records being played, the different beats conflicting. There was also the boom, swish, whee, of games machines working flat out.

'Come on, then!' said Skinny. 'What you waiting for?'

Toby and Fats hung back.

'Five Free Tokens,' said Fats, and frowned. 'That's bad.'

'I don't see why,' said Toby, who felt so sore and mixed up that he took the opposite point of view to Fats out of sheer contrariness.

'It gives them a taste for playing the machines, and then they can't stop.'

'Of course you can stop when you want.'

12

'Ah, but you don't, do you? You go on and on. They'll be losing all their pocket money.'

'Oh, don't be so . . . so wet! I'm going in.'

Toby marched into the arcade. The big scruffy man was standing at the back, doling out tokens to newcomers. He stamped the back of your hand when he'd given you the tokens, so you couldn't cheat and go back twice. Toby didn't like his hand being stamped, but he wasn't going to chicken out, not with Fats hanging around outside with a face like Doomsday.

There were all sorts of machines, with winking lights and noises, and laser beams and bangs, all of them whizzing away like mad. You could go hunting gangsters with laser guns, and kill the baddies – and try not to get hit yourself. You could drive a racing car on a track full of exploding hazards, or be chased by monsters or ghosts or test your reactions by shooting down the Darth Vadar look-alikes. There were so many games going on, Toby felt bewildered.

There were lots of youngsters – mostly boys – already at the machines. Toby went down the aisle to the only vacant one, a simple one-armed bandit in a corner. He'd played on fruit machines a couple of times before, but never won anything.

He didn't win anything with his first three tokens. He thought, easy come, easy go. Then he got two goodies lined up and would you believe it, the third one slid round into place, too! He could hardly believe it! A torrent of tokens gushed out of the slot at him.

He'd hit the jackpot!

2

Toby tried to hold the tokens back, but they kept on coming.

'Hey, what you doing?' said the big man, pushing through the throng to Toby's side. 'What sorta scam you running, then?'

'Don't be daft!' said Toby, shocked. He tried to gather up the tokens in his hands, but there were too many. 'It just happened, that's all.'

'This machine's out of order!' said the man, slapping a notice on it. 'Got to be checked before you can use it again. Sometimes they get temperamental, when they've been moved.'

'You mean it shouldn't have paid off so much?'

'Too right it . . . I mean . . . well, of course, it does happen . . . but . . . ah, well. I suppose it's all good publicity.' He rounded on Red and Skinny, who had rushed up, thrilled to see how much Toby had won. 'Never seen a winner, before? Well, now you have. Honest Joe always gives a fair deal. But this machine's out of order, see. Pick another machine, lad. Enjoy yourself.'

'I can't today,' said Toby. 'I've got to go, or I'll be late.'

Honest Joe was standing in Toby's way. 'You don't want to go yet. Not when you're on a winning streak. Eh, lads? You don't want him to go yet, do you?'

'No, a course not,' said Red, and Skinny agreed. 'Play some more, Toby. I've used up all my money on the Ghost Scare game. It's brill! Lend us some money, and I'll pay you back tomorrow.'

'Here's five each,' said Toby, giving them the tokens. 'But I have to be going, honest. I've got the key, and Mum expects me to get the tea on before Nikki gets back from swimming.'

'You'll be back later, though, won't you?' said Honest Joe, trying on a smile. Smiles didn't look natural on his face.

'Not tonight,' said Toby. 'Can you change the tokens back to money for me?'

'Keep the tokens. Handier for when you come back.'

'I'd rather have the money.'

'Just have one more go, eh? One for the road.'

Toby backed away. The more Honest Joe pressed him to play, the less he wanted to do so. Joe shrugged, and counted out some money into Toby's hands. Toby had a suspicion he'd been short-changed, but he didn't know how much money each token represented, so he said nothing. He just wanted to get away with his winnings. Why, with this money, he could buy, well, anything!

He ran out, leaving Honest Joe to glower after him.

'Lost it all?' said Fats, leaning against a lamp-post.

'I won!' said Toby. He wasn't sure, but he rather thought the machine had paid out more than it was meant to, but he didn't want to let on, not with Fats coming on so superior.

'Oh. Well. I waited for you.'

'Yes.' Toby felt a certain diffidence about his win. How could he share his excitement with Fats, knowing that Fats disapproved?

'I was thinking,' said Fats, swinging his bag. 'What with the church here being out of bounds and all. Would you fancy coming along with mum and me and the kids

15

on Sunday to our church, over the other side of the shopping centre?'

Toby hesitated. Fats had never offered to take him to his church before. It was a long way away, and Toby had planned to do some photography that Sunday. It wasn't as if their own church was open, or the doc would be around to have one of his sessions about the real meaning of life, and how to make the best of it. The doc was all tied up with his move, and anyway, he'd said he was going to another church for the time being. Toby didn't know where. So Toby could go with Fats, if he wanted.

But he couldn't think about anything except the money he'd won. Why, he could buy a personal stereo, or maybe there'd be enough even for a second-hand video, and then he could watch all the things he'd wanted to see that the better-off kids boasted about.

'Toby!' It was Nikki, screeching at him from across the road. It must be later than he thought and she'd got back from swimming before he'd had a chance to get home and start cooking some food.

'Coming!' he yelled back, and dived through a gap in the traffic to the other side.

Toby unlocked the door and Nikki shot up the stairs to the flat. Toby looked at the door of the abandoned surgery. There was a drift of rubbish in the doorway already.

Then he looked back across the road, remembering that he'd parted from Fats without saying goodbye.

But Fats had gone.

As Toby fished some food out of the deep freeze and put it in the microwave, Nikki grumbled about everything. One of her friends had scraped her arm in the swimming baths, she'd lost a sock in the changing room, her class teacher had been in a foul mood, they'd got

16

extra maths for homework. And then the move! Life was pure Grotsville.

Toby thought winning the jackpot would make all the difference, if they had to move. How much would a second-hand video cost? There was one in the pawnbroker's down the road. He said, 'Oh, shut up!'

'You don't need to take your bad temper out on me!'

'I wasn't. It was you who . . .'

'Stop it, you two!' It was their mother's voice. She was home early, and what was more, the doc was with her. He was still in his boiler suit, and looked as if he needed a good wash. He was permanently overworked and overtired, and because his hair was so dark, he often looked as if he hadn't shaved, when he had, really.

He touched Toby's shoulder, grinned at Nikki, and sank into a chair. 'Coffee?' he said, hopefully.

Kate Webb threw the switch on the kettle, and checked that Toby had the right setting on the microwave. She was frowning, and she'd only been half-hearted when she'd told them off for quarrelling. Toby thought they'd better not ask if she'd had any luck at the Town Hall, so he asked the doc if his move had gone all right.

'What? Oh. Yes. Chaos, of course. My nurse threatened to resign at half past four. Couldn't find anything. But yes, it'll be good when we've sorted it all out.'

Kate was staring into space, letting the kettle boil dry. Toby reached over and clicked the kettle off, making coffee for the adults, and tea for himself and Nikki.

The doc said to Toby and Nikki, 'I heard you got your notice to quit today. I was telling your mother, if you go to court, you can get an extension of time.'

'I don't want an extension,' said Kate. 'I hate things being undecided. I don't want to live like that. I want things to be settled.'

'My offer stands,' said the doc, watching her.

Kate pushed her fingers up through her hair. 'Yes, I know, but . . . Toby, Nikki, haven't you any homework to do? Gareth, bring your coffee next door while we wait for the food . . .'

They went into the sitting-room and closed the door.

'At least she's calling him "Gareth" instead of "That Man!" ' said Toby.

'I wonder what sort of offer he made her,' said Nikki. 'A loan? Enough money to buy a flat of our own?'

The phone rang in the hall. Kate got to it before Nikki and shut the kitchen door, so the twins couldn't hear what was going on. They felt left out of things, and they didn't like it.

Their mum was on the phone for quite a while and when she and the doc came out to the kitchen for supper, they were both very quiet. The twins could tell they hadn't resolved their problem, whatever it was. Kate gave a toast in orange juice, 'To the new health centre'.

The doc replied, 'To the future!'

'Something else new,' said Nikki, forking in lasagne as if she hadn't eaten for a week. 'Arcade. Fruit machines. Opposite.'

'That's all I need!' said their mother. 'As if I haven't enough trouble on my plate!'

'Why is it trouble?' enquired Nikki.

'You don't know the problems such places can cause. I wonder how they got a licence for it.'

'The council's pleased to have anyone take a short lease on these properties,' said the doc, with a sigh.

'Jeff should have told me about it. Whatever happens, kids, I don't want to hear of you going in there.'

'Why not?' said Nikki. 'It's good fun.'

The doc said, making a joke of it, 'Good *grief*, more like. Those places separate you from your money quicker than the tax man.'

Toby opened his mouth to say he'd won quite a lot of money there, and closed it again. He didn't want to invite trouble, and he could see his mum was ready to let fly at anything that moved.

'But it's exciting,' argued Nikki, 'and if I lose my own money, then so what?'

'Some ways of getting excitement can permanently damage your health,' said the doc. 'Like cigarettes, and horror movies. I think those machines are addictive, which means . . .'

'I know what it means,' said Nikki, getting angry. 'I'm not going to turn into a gambler, and I don't see why I shouldn't spend my pocket money any way I choose. Can I have some more lasagne?'

'Please!' reminded Kate. 'Toby, you're not hungry?'

Toby shook his head. He didn't like the way the conversation was going. How could he own up to having hit the jackpot when the doc was taking such a strong line? His school bag slumped on the floor, heavy with coins. He hadn't even counted them yet.

'What I mean is,' said the doc, 'that you kids have probably got too much sense to lose more than you can afford, but some of your friends may not be able to stop when they should.'

'Well, I don't see why they shouldn't,' said Nikki. 'I mean, you can't spend more than you've got, can you?'

The doc fiddled with his fork, turning something over in his mind. 'Well, Nikki, it's like this. Some of these places are OK, and make sure youngsters don't go over the top. Some of them even have an age limit. But some don't. Some encourage youngsters to spend more than they've got.'

'So their parents have to stump up,' said Nikki, shrugging.

'Now don't you come to me asking for extra!' said their mum.

'Yes, sometimes it's that,' said the doc. 'And some-times it's . . . oh, maybe I'm slandering the man. But I know no good of him, or his mother.'

'The man's got a mother?' said Nikki, all sarcasm.

'Yes,' said the doc, grinning. 'Joe Clark's got a mother, and she runs a mobile snack bar. I hear she wants to bring it onto the Wasteland, to serve the work-men on the building site.'

'Sounds a good idea,' said Kate. 'Why are you against it?'

The doc sighed. 'It's an old story, and a particularly nasty one. Perhaps it's best forgotten. I'm sure if you kids are sensible, you'll come to no harm. I just wish this hadn't happened when I'm leaving. Which reminds me . . .' he looked at his watch. 'Thanks for the food. I must get back to the health centre. Kate, I wanted to take you out on Friday, but what with the move . . . can I ring you?'

'Sure.' She went with him to the door. Toby and Nikki stopped clearing away to listen to the murmur of voices on the landing. Perhaps Kate realised they were listening, because she went down the stairs with the doc to see him off.

'I wish he'd make her an offer she couldn't refuse,' said Nikki.

'What sort's that?' said Toby.

'Oh, you are dumb!' cried Nikki, and swung off to do her homework.

Toby grabbed his school bag and hauled it up to his room in the attic. The mist had cleared, and the tower was silhouetted against the sky. There was a lot of red in that sky, enough to hope for a fine day tomorrow. Down below, the builders had switched on their lights; they would continue to grab bites out of the earth for quite a while yet. Toby looked down, and the earth swooped up at him.

He was accustomed to looking down on the Wasteland, but now everything looked different. Instead of familiar lumps of masonry, patches of weeds and hard-beaten earth, there was a deep depression in the ground. The builders would not need to excavate right up to Toby's wall because about one third of the site was going to be a small playground and public garden. But even that third of the site was fast disappearing under planks, girders, cement mixers, and Portakabins for offices and loos.

All the old, familiar landmarks had been wiped out. Even as Toby watched, another giant lorry trundled off the site, shaking down the great mound of earth and clay on its back.

Something else was happening. Two men were taking down a section of the hoarding that surrounded the site. A huge silver canister of a caravan waddled its way off the street and took up a position on the Wasteland almost directly under Toby's window. Toby almost fell out of his window with excitement.

A stout figure in a man's anorak and jogging trousers looked up, and saw Toby. It was a woman, wearing a man's cap on her head. She stared at him. He waved at her, but she didn't wave back. A man with a bald head got out of the driving seat of the caravan and joined her. They did something complicated to the side of the caravan, and lo and behold! It was transformed into a mobile café.

One side of the caravan split into two horizontally. The woman and the man with the bald head lowered the bottom part, which was hinged to the bottom of the caravan, and that made a floor. Then they lifted up the top part, which was hinged to the roof of the caravan, and propped it up with great metal struts which fitted into sockets in the 'floor'. That formed the roof of the café.

Toby leaned out, trying to see what was happening under the canopy of the café. Lights were switched on inside, and someone started frying sausages. Three site workers came up, and bought themselves cups of tea and sandwiches and hot dogs. Someone switched on a radio.

As the sky darkened, the caravan seemed an oasis of comfort and light in the Wasteland.

Across the road, the arcade was doing good trade, too. Mother and son, the doc had said. He'd also hinted that he knew something bad about them. Toby thought, 'Well, I don't care what they've done in the past. They're just what we need, now.'

He sat down to count the money he'd won.

3

'Forty-three, forty-four . . .' Toby counted the last coin out of his school bag onto the bed. Forty-four pounds was not enough to buy even a second-hand video. It made him angry to think of having got so much money, but not enough.

He kicked the bed, and some of the coins jerked off onto the floor. He scrabbled after them, wondering how soon he could go back and try to get some more money out of the machine. There wasn't any other way to get what he wanted. His pocket money wouldn't get there, if he saved for a million years.

He would take five pounds . . . and what a lot of money that had seemed only that morning! But now, well, it was just something to buy tokens with, and then he'd go on and on till he got another win.

He could hear Nikki thumping her way up the stairs. He pulled the pillow over the coins, and lay on it, pretending to be looking out into the night.

'Our friendly neighbourhood councillor, Jeff the Beard, has arrived,' announced Nikki, bursting into the room. 'He's brought us prezzies, but don't get excited, it's just a sheet of stickers. Mine are ducks. Ducks! Can you imagine? Yours are cars, or something. I don't think he's realised we're practically teenagers. Oh, and Red's downstairs, wants to see you, but won't come in. Mum said would you deal with him, as the front door's open and letting in a draught.'

Nikki peeled a yellow duckling sticker off the backing paper and pasted it on the door.

'Don't do that,' said Toby. 'You can't get them off.'

'Yes, you can,' said Nikki, peeling it off, and then putting it on again. 'See? And you'd better hurry, Mum says. She's not in too good a mood.'

Toby was worried about leaving his money on the bed under the pillow. Nikki wouldn't look. Probably. She had no idea he had anything to hide. But . . .

'Come on down with me, and see what he wants?'

'OK. I want to watch the new serial on the telly, but Mum's in there with the Beard.'

If they had a video, they wouldn't need to worry about missing programmes.

'Toby!' That was his mum, screeching for him. He elbowed Nikki out of the room. His mum was on the first floor landing, pointing down the stairs. 'Draught!' she said, meaning, Do something about it, quick!

Nikki went into the living room and Toby went down the stairs. Red was standing on the doorstep, shifting from one foot to the other.

'Why didn't you come in?' said Toby.

'Can't. Skinny's waiting for me, over the road. The thing is, we know you won a lot of money, and we're both skint now, used up our free tokens and our pocket money and all. So we wondered if you could lend us some, just till the weekend.'

The perils of winning! thought Toby. He'd already given them five tokens each, and if he gave them more money, they'd pass the word around, and he'd have the whole school wanting to borrow from him. He couldn't risk that.

On the other hand, Red and Skinny were his friends, and he didn't have enough for the video, so he might as well lend to them.

'Promise to give it me back, Friday?'

Red was nodding like a mandarin doll. 'Cross my heart!'

Toby hesitated. 'Look, if I do lend you some, you won't tell anyone else, will you? I know it looked a lot, but when I counted it up, it wasn't as much as I'd thought. I think perhaps he short-changed me . . .'

'If you're so mean that you . . .'

'No, it isn't that. Hold on a mo.'

Toby ran upstairs, and counted out five pounds. A pound each for Red and Skinny, and three for himself to play with. He shovelled all the rest of the coins into the pillow case and dumped it at the head of the bed. No-one would guess what secrets the pillow hid, to look at it.

He gave Red two pound coins. Red ran off across the street without so much as a thank you. Toby felt the satisfying weight of the remaining coins in his hand, and longed to go with him. He could imagine the machine's handle within his grasp, the clatter and clash and the brilliant lights fluttering around him, all screaming for attention. Fire! Bang! Bash! Whee! Jackpot!

'Toby!' His mum was going into overdrive. She'd kill him if she knew what he'd been thinking. Toby shut the front door, leaning against it to shoot the bolt home. Only that way could you be sure to keep the draught out.

Up the stairs and into the living-room. The Beard, Councillor Jeff, had commandeered the one comfortable armchair, with his legs stretched out. Nikki had taken advantage of the wait to turn the telly on, and was crouched close to it with the sound turned low. She'd stuck a duck on the bottom right hand corner of the screen.

'Ah, Toby!' The Beard had a fruity voice, which sounded false on or off the platform. He held out his hand to Toby, who avoided it by sitting on the end of the settee.

The Beard held out a sheet of stickers to Toby. 'Got a little present for you. I know how you boys like cars.' Under his mum's eye, Toby took the sheet and muttered a thank-you. He'd never been interested in cars. Nikki was poised to stick another of her ducks on the side of the telly, by the on/off switch. It was a second-hand job, that telly. One day they'd have a huge colour job. But until they won the pools, they'd manage with this one. Not that they actually did the pools anyway.

'Good news,' said the Beard, giving them a wide-open smile. 'Your mother hasn't said anything?'

'No, of course I haven't,' snapped Kate. 'I told you, I haven't made up my mind yet.'

'Well, I think they have a right to know . . .'

'Nikki, turn the telly off!'

'But I want to watch . . .'

'At once! And take those stupid . . . I mean, take the ducks off the telly, now, this minute, or they'll have to be removed with a knife.'

'No, they won't!' said Nikki.

'As I was saying,' the Beard lifted his voice to drown them out, 'the children have a right to know what their future could be . . .'

Nikki turned the sound down, but kept half her attention on the flickering screen.

'Your mother thinks I could have prevented your being turned out of this flat, but that's not true. The council approved plans for the redevelopment of this block years ago. The developer's budget is limited, and I thought they were going to tackle some other problem sites first, but because of the disturbances to the mains and putting in new sewers on the church site, it's cheaper to do this one now. That's why I didn't try to stop it.'

'Traitors used to have their heads chopped off,' said

Nikki, in a high, sing-song voice, 'and then they put their heads on spikes on Tower Bridge.'

The Beard's colour deepened, and Kate bent down to retie the laces on her trainers.

'So,' said the Beard, 'what I propose is . . .'

Nikki said, 'You mean, you've actually proposed to Mum?'

'No, of course not!' said their mum, hurriedly.

The Beard said, also hastily, 'No, no. You've got me all wrong. I'm not asking your mother to tie herself down in an out-moded contract. Kate's a free spirit, and I'm a free spirit, and I hope we're both adult enough to enter freely into a relationship which will bring positive advantages, with none of the . . .'

Nikki waggled her eyebrows at Toby, meaning, Who's he kidding?

It sounded like a load of old rubbish to Toby, too.

Kate broke in. 'What Jeff means is that he wants us to move in with him, into his big flat. He wants to share it with us, for us to be one unit financially, but to be free to express our personalities without the restraining bonds of, well, of matrimony.'

Nikki said, 'I didn't *think* he meant to marry you!' and turned the sound up on the telly.

'Turn that off, Nikki!' yelled Kate.

Nikki turned it off, and got her trinket box down from the shelf to fiddle with. She was opting out of the conversation and didn't care who knew it.

Kate was breathing hard. 'Listen, twins. There's lots of advantages in Jeff's plan. No strings, for a start. He's got a lovely big flat, fully furnished. We could move in tomorrow, if we liked. A big colour telly, stereo, video. All that sort of thing. And there's more, a lot more.' She turned to Jeff. 'Look, I'll talk to them, tell them everything. I know you've got a meeting . . .'

'Half an hour ago!' said the Beard, leaping to his feet.

'I'll ring you later tonight, then?'

'Yes. Looking forward,' said Kate, seeing him out.

Nikki turned the telly on again. 'I thought he'd never go!'

Kate came back into the room, switched the telly off, and stood in front of it so that Nikki couldn't reach the on/off switch any more.

Kate lit herself a cigarette. 'Listen, kids. Council of War. I won't do anything without your agreement, but I want you to take a good look at what's on the table before you decide.'

Toby said, feeling awkward, 'Mum, you know what we think of him.'

Nikki said, 'He's a creep. He wants you to live with him: oh yes. He wants you to put your salary in with his. He'd get a live-in cook and housekeeper, and we'd have to be polite to him, and say 'thank you' for every little thing. Nothing doing.'

'You don't understand!' said their mum. 'Lots of people think as he does about marriage, and sharing flats and things. There's nothing wrong in it.'

'Nothing right, either,' said Nikki.

'Well, I like him,' said their mum, 'and I think that a lot of what he says makes sense.' She rubbed her forehead as if she had a headache coming. 'Listen, kids. It isn't as simple as you make out. I'm fond of Jeff. He's kind, and well, it's not easy, bringing you two kids up by myself. There've been times when I've almost given up. You've got years more of schooling, and then maybe polytechnics, or universities. It all stretches out into the future, and when you're a single mother on your own . . . well, it's daunting.

'Jeff wants to help, and the kind of help he can give us, well, it could make all the difference to you getting good A levels. He knows of a boarding school which offers bursaries to disadvantaged children, and he thinks he can get you in. I'd hardly have anything to pay for a first-class education, and you'd be set up for life.'

Toby and Nikki stared at Kate, and she stared at the floor. Finally she said, in a sad voice, 'You see? It's not so simple, is it? I mean, I'd do anything for you kids, you know that. Anything.'

Toby and Nikki looked at one another. As twins they often fooled outsiders because they didn't look alike, but on this issue they thought as one.

'Tell him no deal,' said Nikki. 'And we're not disadvantaged. We're OK.'

'Honest, Mum, it wouldn't work.'

'Why not?' said Kate, fighting a losing battle.

'You know why not,' said Nikki. 'He's not our sort.'

Toby said, 'We can get good results from this school, if we work hard. There's a boy from our school went to Oxford last year, and two to London University, and lots to polys and things.'

'And,' said Nikki, 'there's someone *we* like better.'

'I don't know what you mean!' said Kate, but she went red, so they didn't believe her.

'Just what did the doc offer?' asked Toby.

Kate yelled, 'Mind your own business!' and whirled out of the room.

Toby said, 'You don't want to go to boarding school, do you, Nikki?'

'I wouldn't mind, if everything else was right. But you'd hate it, wouldn't you?'

'Yes,' said Toby.

'So that's all right, then.' Nikki leaned forward to stick the last duck on the underside of the telly, switched it on, and turned the sound up. Toby remembered that he hadn't found a hiding place for his money yet, and went upstairs to do something about it.

4

Once a week the comprehensive school had Assembly time. First they had the notices and then the obligatory pep talk. It was Technical Drawing next, and Toby quite liked that, so he was peeved when they didn't move out afterwards. Suddenly Mr McDonald, the deputy head, strode in, tagging a policeman in his wake.

Red sniggered. 'Uh-uh! What you bin up to, then, Skinny?'

Skinny looked peaky. Skinny had almost been drawn into his much older brother's gang of muggers last year, and it hadn't been kind of Red to remind him of it.

'Good morning, everyone.' The usual guff, introducing the police.

Then it got interesting, because the policeman was talking about something local. There'd been a spate of thefts from cars and houses and flats around the shopping centre. Videos, radio sets, tellies, that sort of thing; cash and jewellery as well. The police had 'reason to believe' that someone local was buying the stuff from the burglars.

Toby looked along the line of his friends, all gazing blankly at the policeman. It was obvious none of them had heard any of such goings-on around their way. With Mike and his gang in prison, life had been pretty quiet of late around Paradise Row. Of course, the shopping centre was some way off, and although some people from school lived out that way, none of Toby's lot did.

The policeman said he wanted them all to be on the look-out, and to report anything suspicious at once.

'It's better to be on the safe side,' he said. 'Don't wait to ask the burglar if he has a right to break into a neighbour's flat. Sprint for the nearest phone and dial for help. Don't be fooled by his or her youth; some of the burglaries and most of the rip-offs from cars, have been carried out by kids as young as eight years old.'

There was a Phew! from some of the school, but a lot of the kids nodded or looked self-conscious, so Toby reckoned the policeman knew what he was talking about.

Later, in the playground, Red and Skinny came up to Toby with a couple of their friends. They wanted to borrow some more money. The story of Toby's jackpot win had spread, and they regarded him with a mixture of envy and greed.

'Come on, Toby. Let us have a few pounds, you can spare it, easy!'

'No, I don't have enough to . . .' began Toby.

'We know you won maybe fifty pounds,' Red said.

'I can't wait to get back on the Racing Track game,' said Skinny. 'Whee! You can alter the speed, and it's just like flying, you go so fast . . .'

'I like the Missile Show one best . . .'

'We didn't know you could win so much on the machines. Me brother said they was all fixed not to pay out much, but you did win, so sucks to big brother, and I'm going to have another go tonight.'

Toby said, 'Now look, I was just lucky . . .'

'So I can get lucky, too. I've got my lucky charm with me, today. All I need is a coupla pounds to start.'

Now Toby had brought five pound coins with him, intending to do the same thing. He didn't feel rich yet. He felt as if he'd just got one foot on the ladder of success, and he didn't want to be pushed off it by the others. Yet he couldn't refuse them, not with everyone knowing he'd won so much.

'OK,' said Toby. 'I did win, but not all that much. It just looked a lot, that's all.'

'Oh, har, har. Listen to 'im. Wants us to believe he's skint!'

Nikki and her friends came up. They'd heard about his win, too. Nikki was livid with him. 'You rotten thing, why didn't you tell me about winning a hundred pounds? You could at least have given me some money this morning, so's I could play, too!'

Toby said, 'It was nowhere near that, and anyway, Mum said . . .'

'So what! You're a fine brother, cheating your twin like this!'

Toby pulled his pockets inside out, and showed them that he only had five coins on him. He kept one back for himself, but had to give the rest up. No-one was satisfied with their share, least of all Nikki, who said she wanted half of what he'd won as soon as they got back home.

Toby went off to grouch by himself. He didn't see why he should have to give his winnings away. It was his money, wasn't it? Not theirs. The fact was that they just weren't lucky, like him. Skinny had been on another fruit machine, and said he'd won two tokens on his fourth try, but he'd lost them again. So, tough!

The others preferred the excitement of the action games which didn't even pretend to give you anything back. You put your money in, got your big thrill for a couple of minutes and that was it.

Toby told himself that he didn't know how they could just throw good money after bad. He wasn't like that. He played to win, and not for kicks.

There were far more games machines than there were fruit machines. Toby wondered why. Did more people prefer them? Or were they a better money earner for the arcade?

Suppose it were true that fruit machines were fixed not to pay out much? Honest Joe's reaction to Toby's win certainly seemed to bear that out. If so, then the machine which had given him the jackpot would by now have been fixed not to do so again, and Toby's chances of winning anything substantial were pretty remote.

He put that thought aside. He didn't want it to be true. He wanted to believe he could win and win again.

'Hi!' said Fats, hitting Toby on the back.

'Ouch! You don't know your own strength.'

'Sorry. Just thought I'd tell you, I've got football practice after school. Come and watch?'

'What, watch the All Blacks at play?'

Toby hadn't meant it to sound snide, but as the words came out, he realised they could have been better chosen. Fats gave him a wise-eyed stare, and walked off without another word.

There goes my best friend, thought Toby, but he made no effort to go after him. He'd make it up with Fats later. Or perhaps he wouldn't bother. He had better things to do with his time than hang around waiting for a football fanatic to turn back into a proper friend who had time to spend with him.

After school Toby and Nikki and their friends raced out of school and along to the arcade. There were lots of other young people there already. Toby recognised some of the older pupils from school. They were mostly boys, and a lot bigger and tougher than Toby and his friends.

Nikki managed to commandeer the biggest and loudest games machine of the lot, and got her friend Jan to help her sort out the rules. Her reactions were quick and she managed to explode almost all the baddies who were gunning down her secret agent. She only gave up her place when her money ran out and a big boy threatened to stomp her one if she didn't shift. She yelled at Toby to bring her some more money, but he pretended not to hear.

Toby had gone straight to his old 'friend' the fruit machine in the corner. He caressed the cold, shiny surface. This was his 'good luck' machine. This machine had given him a lot of money yesterday, money that he was going to use to make their life bearable in the future. Toby thought, 'After I get the video, I'm going to get a colour telly, and then maybe I'll get a new camera, with automatic focus, and different lens . . .'

Skinny came breathing down his neck. 'Well, are you going to play, or aren't you? Red's on the Monsters machine and won't let me in. I'm going to pay him back by winning on this one, and then when he's run out of money, I'm going to laugh and tell him to get lost. I'm going to win enough to play all night, if I want to.'

Toby couldn't concentrate with Skinny crowding in. He wanted to be alone with the machine, to talk to it, to coax it into giving him more money. So he stood back and let Skinny have first go. Skinny crooned 'Be Lucky!' to himself, pounded his token in, and started working the handle. He jumped up and down as the rolls turned round, hesitated, and stopped. Skinny scowled at the row of assorted fruit, and put in another coin.

'Don't watch me like that!' Skinny complained. 'How can I play with you staring at me?'

Toby turned away. He watched Red trying to steer a baby monster through a haunted house, trying to avoid other, larger monsters as he went. The noise was deafening. The flickering lights from the machines were reflected in the boys' eyes as they clung to the knobs, mouths gaping, tongues flickering . . .

'I won!' screeched Skinny, waving three bright new tokens in his hand. His face was staring white with excitement.

Toby thought, The Thrill of the Kill! That's what it's all about!

Nikki was crowding Skinny as he fed his token back into the fruit machine. He swore at her for jogging his arm. Red's last token ran out and the machine blared at him, *Now put in another token to keep the game going before the countdown ends . . . ten . . . nine . . . eight . . .*

Red kicked the machine. He hadn't any more money, and a large man was waiting to take over.

'Toby, lend us some more!'

'I can't . . .'

Skinny, without even asking, seized the tokens from Toby, and fed them into the fruit machine, working the handle like a maniac. 'You gotta get a rhythm going,' he kept saying. 'Come on, come on!'

The machine sent back two tokens in exchange for the five which Skinny had put in. He yelled, 'I've won!'

Toby thought, why didn't I tell him to push off? It's *my* machine. Why did I let him have the tokens? Because he lost all his money yesterday? Because I feel guilty about having won when all the others have lost? Because all this violence bothers me?

'Oh, fishcake!' said Nikki, scowling and stamping. 'I want to play, too. Toby, lend us . . .'

'Haven't got any more.'

'Of course you have!'

'You've had the lot. Search me, if you don't believe me!'

Red pushed between them. 'Toby, you've got to lend me . . .'

'He's broke,' said Nikki, impatiently. 'Oh, come on. I've got some pocket money still at home. I'll go and get it. Coming, Jan?'

Toby went with them. He'd divided up his winnings before he'd gone to bed and hidden them in three places in his bedroom. One lot was wrapped in newspaper and pushed under a loose floorboard, another was behind some of the books in his bookcase, and the third he'd left as a float, rolled in some socks in his cupboard.

'I've got 75p,' said Nikki, toiling up the stairs to Toby's room. 'Let's have a look at what you won, Toby?'

'This is it,' said Toby, unrolling his socks, and showing them. It looked quite a lot, lying there on his hand. In fact, it was only fifteen pounds.

'Is that all?' said Red. 'It can't be!'

'Well, I . . .'

'You mean, you went back last night and played with the rest, and lost it? Oh, I don't believe it! All that money!'

Toby jumped at the suggestion. If he could only make them believe he'd lost the rest, perhaps they'd leave him alone. It was still a lot of money, fifteen pounds. It meant a big proportion of the new video. He didn't want them to have it. He could feel his hand trying to close around the coins.

'Seven fifty for me, and seven fifty for you,' said Nikki, taking eight pound coins, and giving him 50p change.

'And you'll lend me a couple,' said Skinny, taking it for granted. 'That's . . . how many I owe you?'

'Same for me,' said Red. 'I simply gotta get back to that machine. Wow, is it wicked?'

Toby looked at his hand. There was three pounds fifty left for him. Out of fifteen pounds. It wasn't much. He was only thankful he hadn't told them about the rest of the money that he'd hidden.

They scampered down the stairs and across the street into the Arcade. The big man gave them a crocodile grin, and changed their money into tokens. There were a lot of people playing the machines now, and some hanging around, waiting for a turn. The fruit machine in the corner was hidden from view by three large boys

36

from the top of their school. There wasn't a hope of getting near it. Toby made up his mind to wait patiently, and not get sidetracked into losing his money on another machine.

'I got him, Pow!' screeched Nikki, jumping up and down. But all too soon she was elbowed away from the machine by a man.

'How did Toby win on this machine?' screeched Skinny, furious at having lost yet again.

"Seasy!' said Nikki. 'You just use your loaf, like this . . .' She put a token into the fruit machine, and lost it. And four more.

'Ho, ho!' said Skinny, sarcastically. 'So that's how it's done, is it? How many you got left?'

'Two. Leave me alone!' She fed one in, and lost it.

'Give us one.'

'No. Get your own.' Nikki evaded his hand to put her last token in. The machine pipped and winked at her, and swallowed the token. She kicked it, and hopped up and down on a bruised foot. 'Ouch! Horrible thing! I don't like playing on this one, anyway. Just wait till I can get back on "Licensed to Kill"!'

Red came jigging up. 'Wow, what a marvellous game! It's ace, it's brill, it's . . . magnetic!'

Toby got to 'his' machine. He could feel them all watching. It made the skin crawl up the back of his neck. He put in a token, and tried to concentrate, to will the machine to pay off, but it was no good. He lost. He played again and again, working himself into a frenzy. But it was no good. He lost the lot without getting even one token back.

He looked round at Nikki and his friends. They were all wearing the same defeated look. He shrugged, and led the way out into the street. As the door fell to behind them, the noise was cut off, as if with a knife. They were back in everyday life.

Toby felt sick. Fifteen pounds, he thought. I can hardly believe it, but I've gone and lost fifteen pounds! That's pocket money for ever.

'Toby, are you sure you haven't any more . . . ?'

Toby pulled his pockets out, to show they were empty. Perhaps he could get back later on, when it was quieter, and he could concentrate, and then he'd see what luck really was.

Red kicked a Coke tin along the pavement. Nikki and Jan and Skinny argued about who they could borrow from.

'Look!' said Toby, pointing.

There was a screech of tyres, and a police car drew up outside the arcade. Three large men went in, and stopped everybody leaving.

'Wow!' cried Nikki. 'It's a raid!'

5

Toby, Nikki and their friends watched from a safe distance, while the police turned over the Den of Delights.

A second unmarked police car arrived, and two more men went into the arcade. The door was shut, locked, and a blind pulled down over the windows. If you had crowded close to the door, you might have been able to see what was going on inside, but nobody felt that curious. In dribs and drabs, the customers were let out and went off cursing, or looking pale.

'Looking for drugs?' guessed Red.

'Nah,' said Skinny. 'It's only been open two minutes. How could they be pushing drugs already?' Skinny was acknowledged to have had a better education in the under-world than the others.

Nikki said, jogging up and down. 'I hope they're not going to close the place. It's the most exciting thing that's happened for ages.'

Toby thought, I wonder if that fruit machine *was* fixed, and the police found out.

Nikki shrieked, 'Look at the time! Mum'll be home in a minute and we haven't got the supper started!'

The others had to go, too. The police remained inside, and the blinds remained down, so there was no point in hanging around anyway.

It was Toby's turn to cook the supper while Nikki cleaned the place up, so he got a pie out of the freezer and put it in the microwave, while Nikki tackled the dust in the living-room. Every now and then one or the other of them would dart to the window to see what was happening across the road.

Nothing much did.

Their mum came in, and they ate. Neither Toby nor Nikki mentioned the goings-on across the road. They didn't think their mother would appreciate the narrow escape they'd had from being caught in a police raid.

Afterwards, Toby went upstairs to his room. The blinds were up at the arcade, and business seemed to be as usual. There was no sign of the police cars, and the big, heavy man was standing in the doorway, looking as if he'd never had a wicked thought in his life.

Work had continued all this time on the site. They wouldn't stop for something as trivial as a police raid on a shop opposite. The air was heavy with dust. A crane swung a load of girders off the back of a lorry. A man in a hard yellow hat guided the load to a space by the Portakabins. The lorry driver parked at the kerb and joined two or three other men at the café.

Toby craned out of the window. Something was not quite right, but he couldn't make out what it was.

Mrs Clark strode out onto the Wasteland, and stood talking to a couple of tough-looking men. They weren't site workers because site workers all had to wear hard hats. One of the men was completely bald. It was he who'd helped her set up the snack bar. The other one had a thin crop of bright yellow hair and a ginger moustache. It was clear that she was giving orders to Baldy and Yellowtop, and not the other way round.

Mrs Clark was wearing a hard hat, but it wasn't yellow, and it wasn't the same shape as the site workers'. Toby gaped. She'd got an old war-time air-raid warden's helmet, just like the one Toby had in his collection! Toby cherished that hat, because it had belonged to the doc's grandfather, who'd been Air Raid Warden at the church during the war. In those parts, they still spoke of the old Warden with affection.

To his right, Toby saw a pile of scaffolding and girders, and a new shed with a bright new padlock on it. The site was patrolled at night by a guard dog.

The caravan wasn't in the same position as on the previous night. Perhaps that was what was bugging him. It had been manoeuvred to stand parallel to the wall beneath Toby's window, leaving a gap of maybe a metre, a sort of passageway between the wall and the caravan. Someone had boarded over the passageway at just above head height. Perhaps Mrs Clark had set up a portable loo there.

The sun was fading from the sky. The working lights had been switched on all over the site and light poured from the front of the café.

Baldy and Yellowtop were standing by the entrance to the passage behind the café, talking. They looked up at Toby as he leaned out of his window. They didn't give him a friendly wave. In fact, if their stares had been armed, Toby would have dropped out of his window and fallen dead at their feet.

Toby drew back into his room. He couldn't think why the men didn't like him looking down on them, but they didn't.

Nikki came banging into the room and threw herself on the bed beside Toby. 'Before you ask, I've rung round all my friends to ask for a loan, and they wouldn't give me one! I'm in a rotten mood.'

Toby was more interested in what was going on outside. He peered out from behind the curtain. Baldy and Yellowtop were carrying heavy cartons into the café from a delivery van parked on the road.

Nikki said, without much interest, 'What are you looking at?'

'Ma's helpers. They're stocking up with food. Boxes of crisps and stuff from the frozen food shop. They must have some sort of freezer in there, to keep the food at the right temperature. I wonder how they manage for electricity.'

'Caravans do, nowadays. I've got a friend at school whose family's got a mobile home. Everything's in it, including a telly.'

'They've set up their own loo, out the back.'

'What about the arcade?'

'Business as usual. The Den of Delights is fully operational again.'

'Mum says she's been to the Housing Department, and they've said she'll probably get a good flat in the block.'

Toby's stomach took a plunge.

'I ask myself,' said Nikki, 'would it be better to go and live in the flats, or go to boarding school?'

'Flats,' said Toby, 'definitely.'

'Boarding school,' said Nikki. 'If it weren't for Jeff making the offer and you hating the idea.'

'I couldn't stand boarding school, Nikki.'

'I know that, stupid! I told her, No. But she isn't listening. She wants to talk to you about it, all mumsy-wumsy to her ickle boy. I told her you hated Jeff as much as I did, but she wouldn't listen to that, either. I don't know what's got into her. Senile decay, or something.'

'She's just worried about us.'

'We're all right. We can manage. Even if we do have to go and live in those rotten flats.'

'Toby!' That was their mum, fortissimo.

'Coming,' said Toby. He left Nikki lolling all over his bed, and went down to the sitting-room.

His mum was smoking, always a sign of stress with her. She'd been running her fingers through her hair again, and made it as spiky as a punk's. She pointed to the chair and he sat, realising he was in for a lecture, and glancing at the clock. There was something he wanted to watch on telly at eight.

'Now, Toby. I want a straight talk with you. Your sister is being, well, difficult. She can sometimes be rather childish, but I know that you're a lot more mature, and that I can have a sensible talk with you.'

'I don't think it's a good idea for you to move in with Jeff, either. Mum, can't you see how awful he is?'

She went an ugly red. 'Now listen here. I don't have to take that sort of talk from you. What I decide to do with my life is my business. All I want from you is a little cooperation, a little understanding. I know you haven't always got on with Jeff . . .'

'Understatement of the year,' said Toby, hunching his shoulders and trying to make his voice growly.

She ignored that. '. . . but you're old enough now to appreciate what he's prepared to do for you . . .'

'Could you get Nikki into a boarding school, without him pulling strings?'

'Well, I . . . perhaps. But that's not the point.'

'She'd quite like to go to boarding school.'

'It's a package deal, Toby. Jeff's prepared to offer me a home and to have you around in the holidays, but he thinks – and I do agree with him, really – that you two would get a better education, have a better chance in life, if you went to boarding school.'

'In exchange for what?' said Toby.

'Well, really, Toby, that's my business.' She'd gone red again. Toby suddenly couldn't bear to talk about it any more. It was so embarrassing!

He said, 'It's eight o'clock. Can I switch the telly on?'

'No, you can't! We've got to have this out.'

'You know what I think. What's the point of going over it?'

'You are being very stupid about this, Toby. Would I be going into this, without believing it was for the best for all of us?'

Toby tried to hook the nearest chair over with his foot.

'Answer me! Would I?'

Toby shrugged. He didn't know how his mum could even think of moving in with the Horrible Beard. But what could he say that he hadn't said already?

He said, 'The programme's started.'

'You and your telly!' She was going to start yelling at him in a minute. 'If you can't . . .'

Nikki burst into the room. 'Mum, could you lend me a pound till the weekend?'

'Why? You get your pocket money on Fridays and not before.'

'Well, if you must know, I'm hungry. Supper didn't fill me up, and I keep smelling the hot dogs from the caff, and I just thought . . .'

'Why didn't you say? Of course you and Toby can have a hot dog each, though really, kids, I hope you won't make a habit of it, because that sort of junk food's no good for you, you know.' She found her purse and gave them a pound each. Nikki winked at Toby, and he knew she really wanted to dash across to the arcade.

He followed her down the stairs. 'Listen, you wouldn't cheat on her, would you? You do mean to get a hot dog?'

'What's it to you?'

'Just that I don't like seeing her cheated.'

'Oh, all right,' said Nikki. 'I am pretty hungry, anyway.'

'Hey, what are they doing now?' said Toby, as they rounded the corner into the Wasteland.

Some building site workers were fixing tall rolls of wire to posts, cutting off the caravan and a small strip of land in front of it from the building site. You could still get to the caravan from the street, but the site workers would have to go out by one of the official gates and round by the road to get their cuppas in future.

The ghetto-blaster in the café had been turned right up. Puffs of the delectable aroma of fried sausages and onions drifted across the site. The big woman in her tin hat and great white apron looked even larger than the two large construction workers who were drinking cups of tea at the counter.

Toby and Nikki eyed their hot dogs greedily. Toby tried not to eat too fast, because he was burning his tongue. Oh, but they were just fantastic, those hot dogs!

'So what happened next, missus?' said one of the workers.

The big woman leaned forward over the counter. 'So the fuzz didn't find nothing, did they? So they had to apologise, din't they? Egg all over their faces.'

The two men laughed. Toby and Nikki edged closer. Was Mrs Clark talking about the police raid on the arcade?

'My son, he tole them he was going to sue. Sue the pants off them, he said. Breaking and entering, turning the place upside down. Look at the damage, he said. Paintwork. Dents in the machines. Oh, they'll have to pay, and pay through the nose.'

'What were they looking for?'

She shrugged, her chest heaving in one mighty surge. She was a powerfully built woman. Toby thought he wouldn't like to meet her in an alley on a dark night.

'They said they was looking for stolen goods. Prove it, he said. Go on, he said. Just you find one sniff of something dodgy, and I'll come down the nick with you, no fuss, no arguments. But they didn't find nothing and why? 'Cos there was nothing to find.'

The building workers nodded, and smiled down into

their cups of tea. Toby could see them wondering if there really had been anything to find. The big woman flung a tea towel over her shoulder, and it hit the shelf at the back with a 'thuck'. 'What I says is, the fuzz has got too big for their boots. Bursting into people's businesses, and stopping them from earning an honest living. If they had their way, we'd all have to shut up shop. Why, they even tried to stop me parking on this site, only they couldn't. It's public property, and they never knew it. Shows how much good they are, don't it?'

'It used to be a right of way, or something,' said one of the men to the other. 'They're not sure it's still legal, but they're looking into it.'

'Lived around here all me life,' said the woman. 'First in one of them poky houses down the street. Then in the flats. Working all hours, serving in someone else's caff. Then my son Joe he says to me, "Ma, how about I set you up in your own place?" And he bought me this. I was taking it round the markets but the fuzz was always running me off. Then I remembered that this bit of land here used to be a right of way, a passage between the church and the house at the back of us. We always played here when we was children, right up till the bombing. And if it's a right of way, then I have a right to be on it. Right?'

'Right, Mrs Clark,' said one of the men.

'Just call me "Warden",' said the woman, tipping her helmet forward over one eye with a horribly roguish gesture. 'I've even got meself a Warden's hat, see?'

Toby dropped the last mouthful of his hot dog onto the earth.

'What's the matter with you?' hissed Nikki.

'It's all wrong,' muttered Toby. 'She mustn't call herself "Warden".'

'Tell her so, then.'

Toby didn't dare, and she didn't expect him to, either.

'Better go back, I suppose,' sighed Nikki. 'Bags of homework.'

They went round to their front door. While Toby was fishing out the key, Nikki leaned against the door of the empty surgery, kicking at the rubbish that had accumulated there.

Suddenly she shot upright and grabbed Toby's shoulders.

'Listen!' she said in a muffled shriek. 'There's someone in the surgery! Burglars!'

6

'Don't be daft!' said Toby. 'Burglars don't break into empty shops.'

Nikki was not reassured. 'I'm sure there's somebody moving about in there. I heard a sort of scraping and then a bang, as if someone had moved something heavy and then dropped it.'

Toby put his ear to the door, and listened.

'Nothing. You heard something from the building site. There's so much banging and crashing going on there, I'm surprised I could even hear you complain you had too much mustard on your hot dog.'

'I suppose that was it.' But she looked doubtful.

Toby did his Sherlock Holmes/Hawkeye bit. He peered at the lock and the blanked off window. There was nothing to be seen that shouldn't be there.

'The lock's all right. Paint's all right.' He shook the door, and it refused to budge. 'There's so much rubbish in the entrance, you could see if anyone had opened the door.'

'Sure,' said Nikki, reassured, but she still jumped when their own front door opened abruptly. It was only their mum, in the company of the Great Bearded One.

'Hi, kids,' said the Beard.

'Hi,' they returned, without enthusiasm.

'I'm going down the pub with Jeff for a while,' said their mum, who was wearing her new dangly jet earrings.

She had some sort of perfume on, as well. Toby thought, oh yuk! How could she!

'Don't watch telly too late,' she said.

'Don't you monitor what they watch?' said the Beard, speaking to her as if the twins were not present. 'I wouldn't let any kids of mine watch what they pleased . . .'

'Oh, they're pretty sensible on the whole.'

She pecked Nikki on the forehead, touched Toby on the shoulder, and went off with the Beard, who was gesticulating all over the place, and going on about surveys and violence, and peer group pressures and all the stuff that Toby and Nikki found so boring.

'Serve him right if I watch the late night horror film,' said Nikki.

Toby said nothing. Climbing the stairs made his chest feel hard and tight, and at the top he paused to breathe. He was so angry with himself! He hadn't had an attack of asthma all winter. Maybe it was the dust floating around from the building site. He found his old inhaler, where he'd thrown it into the bottom of his cupboard, but it was useless by this time.

He didn't stay up watching telly, but kept to his room, did his homework as best he could, and went to bed, propped up on pillows. The noise from the building site had died down by that time, and it was eerily quiet out there.

Toby couldn't get comfortable in bed. His chest got tighter and tighter, and he heard himself begin to wheeze.

'Lord Jesus, help me,' gasped Toby.

He'd not been thinking much about Jesus recently. He'd had a lot of other things to think about, and somehow Jesus had got pushed to the back of his mind.

Usually he prayed quite a bit, on and off, as he went through the day. And he never went to bed without praying, and reading a bit of the Bible. But all that had been forgotten. It was a shock to him to realise how long it was since he'd thought about it. He felt ashamed that it had taken an attack of asthma to remind him.

He said a short prayer in his head. He couldn't see his Bible on the bed-side table. He remembered now that it had dropped to the floor and been pushed under the bed when he'd been looking for his shoes the other day. He'd fetch it out tomorrow. He heard the front door close, and his mother mounting the stairs. Alone.

He thought of calling out to her, but then he thought she had enough to worry about at the moment, without bothering with his asthma. But she came up to his door, and looked in to see if he was awake. He turned his head, and she came into the room without putting the light on, and sat on his bed.

'Can't sleep?'

He shook his head. He thought she'd hear his breathing was worse, but she was too wound up for that.

She said, 'You know, Jeff's a good man, and he really cares for me. I wish you and Nikki would stop this silly way you have of calling him "The Beard". It's, well, childish, don't you think?'

'Accurate?' murmured Toby.

'He's got feelings, just like anyone else.'

'Like the doc has?' said Toby, hopefully. 'I thought you were supposed to go out with the doc tonight.'

'He cancelled. Some emergency. As Jeff says, I can never rely on . . . well, I suppose he's right.' She sighed. She wasn't looking at Toby, but staring into the dark. He wondered what she saw there. Sometimes he could make out faces in the cracks in the plastered ceiling, but it was too dark for that, and anyway, she was into that sort of fanciful thinking.

'It's late. I must go,' she said, but made no move. She was holding some papers, and now put them on his bedside table. 'Look at those in the morning. They're all about the new school that you're going to. Jeff is fixing an interview.'

Toby felt the rhythm of his breathing break up.

'It's a beautiful place,' she said, still not noticing his asthma. 'Lovely grounds, own swimming pool, playing fields, science block, library, music rooms, everything. Even its own theatre. Fancy that! Your own theatre.'

'Not interested,' said Toby, in a hard, tight voice. He held his hand over his chest to keep it warm. Sometimes that helped.

'Of course you're interested. You're a very lucky boy.'

'I don't want it!' Toby lashed out and shot the pile of literature onto the floor.

She said, 'Don't be like that!' and walked out, leaving the papers where they were. Toby got out of bed, picked them up and tore them into tiny pieces, without reading them. He dropped the bits in his waste-paper basket and then collapsed on the bed, working at his breathing, in, out . . . in, out. Help me, Jesus, please. In, out, please don't let her do this to us!

But it was a long time before he got to sleep.

Next day he went to see the doc at his new health centre. It was in a new building, with doors that opened as you approached. There were two receptionists behind desks, working at computers, and ranks of patients' files in an alcove behind them. The waiting room was kitted out with a play area for toddlers, all bright and shiny with toys. There was a quiet waiting room with a lot of people in it, and a mobile that turned lazily in the upsurge of air from the central heating. There were cheerful pictures on the walls.

'Wow,' thought Toby, sniffing the new paint and newly-sawn wood smells. 'This is something else.'

He gave his name to one of the women behind the

desks. She found his notes and told him to sit down and wait. There were lots of doors leading off the waiting room, with names like, Nurse, X-Ray, Dental Hygiene and so on. Also the names of two doctors. Toby got out his homework and started on it.

At last he was called to go in to the doctor, but it wasn't the right doctor, not *his* doctor. Toby supposed she looked all right, fair-haired and plumpish and efficient, but it was not the same as seeing his old friend. Toby stopped on the threshold.

'Go on,' said the nurse.

'Come in,' said the doctor.

'I have to see my own doctor,' said Toby, backing out.

The doctor and the nurse tutted. The doctor said, 'In this practice, we share everything. Won't you tell me what the trouble is, er, let me have his notes please, nurse?'

'No,' said Toby. 'I don't mean to be rude, but . . .'

'Asthma, is it?' said the doctor, who was a bit sharper than Toby's mum had been. 'Well, I'm sure I can help you with that.'

'No, sorry,' said Toby, wheezing away. 'Got to see Dr. Gareth.'

They stopped smiling. He could see he was disrupting their nice new system. 'I'm afraid he's out,' said the nurse. 'So unless you want to come back tomorrow . . .'

'I'll wait,' said Toby.

'I'm afraid that won't be possible,' said the woman doctor. 'We close in fifteen minutes. Now let me see, about your asthma . . .' Toby turned and blundered out into the street without waiting for a prescription. His breathing was getting worse. He had to see the doc, just had to! He tried to remember where the doc lived. He ought to know, because the doc had had them there for impromptu suppers once or twice.

Toby lifted his head to the steel grey of the sky, and there was the moving finger of the big crane on their building site. And beyond it on the skyline was the silhouette of the flats. Now he knew where he was.

He turned two corners into a quiet square. There was no through traffic, and no buses. The pavements were comparatively clean of rubbish, although you could see people walked their dogs there. Toby saw the doc's car outside his house. So far, so good.

The doc lived in a big house in the middle of a terrace. But the houses here were not like the one Toby lived in. These houses had elbow room. Some had semi-basements, and some were double-fronted. The doc's not only had a double front, but it was one storey higher than the rest. It looked as if it had been built for an important person. It could have done with a coat of paint, but it wasn't shabby the way the houses were in Paradise Row.

Toby knew that the doc had bought his big house when he'd needed to look after his mother in the years before she died. The doc took in lodgers nowadays, partly for the company, and partly because single people often found it difficult to find accommodation.

Toby rang the bell and waited. He wasn't at all sure he ought to have come, but he refused to give in and go home.

The doc came, and Toby saw at once that it was all right. The doc was wearing his old boiler suit, and looked dusty and tired, but he put both his hands on Toby's shoulders, and held him tight.

'I'm glad you came, Toby. They just rang through from the surgery. I hoped you'd come here. I'm going to have to mark certain files so they know I deal with those people personally. Sorry you didn't stay to talk to my new partner. She's first-class, you know.'

'Sure,' said Toby. 'But I wanted to see you.'

The doc drew Toby into the house. The hall looked like a left luggage office. 'My lodgers are leaving tomorrow, going on a round the world trip. Come through into the kitchen.'

The doc more or less lived in the kitchen, which was a big, warm, untidy room at the back of the house. The large window overlooked a garden which was mostly lawn, with a few trees round the edges. Rather an unimaginative garden, Toby thought, for the type of man the doc was.

The doc offered Toby a drink of squash and some biscuits. Toby felt his breathing ease. The doc always had that effect on him.

'Asthma again?' said the doc. 'I half expected it, because of the dust from the building site. You've done pretty well, this last six months, but that dust . . .'

'It's not just the dust,' said Toby. 'It's mum, and Jeff wants us to go and live in his flat and . . .'

'Uh-huh.' The doc looked out of the window.

'. . . and she couldn't go out with you last night, so she went out with Jeff.'

'Mm.' The doc sighed. 'She has every right to go out with him if she wants.'

'You know what he wants to do? He wants to get us out of the way to boarding school. She thinks it's a good idea.'

'From the point of view of your schooling, it probably is. Nikki would find it a great adventure.'

'I wouldn't.'

The doc didn't reply, but pushed the packet of biscuits across. 'You know I wouldn't,' said Toby. 'Besides, I know what that Jeff's like. When we came back in the holidays, he'd make us feel we were in the way. He does it now, so what would it be like then?'

The doc made a sound half-way between a groan and a laugh. 'I don't suppose you two would be the easiest of lodgers.'

'We would, if the person was all right. I mean, if we could live here with you and be your lodgers, we'd be as good as anything.'

The doc stared at the biscuits, and Toby stared at the doc.

The silence went on a bit, and Toby began to think he'd made an awful mistake, and that the doc didn't want them at all.

'Er,' said Toby. 'Sorry. Perhaps I ought to be going now.'

'No, don't go. You're quite right,' said the doc, leaping to his feet, and starting to tackle the mountain of washing-up in the sink. 'Believe me, Toby, there's nothing I'd like better. I was hoping your mother would agree to move into the flat upstairs. It's got its own entrance from the side. I was going to get some decorating done, as soon as my lodgers had gone. I know your mother's worried about your schooling, and if things had been different . . . but there it is.'

'What things?'

The doc suspended operations to stare out of the window. 'It would be very easy to rush things, but that would be wrong, too. You must realise that your mother and I are very fond of one another . . .'

An unexpected joy shot into Toby's mind. 'You mean . . . ?'

'No, I haven't asked her to marry me . . . yet. Your mother is going through a bad time. She likes to have everything clear cut, to know exactly where she stands. At the moment she's confused. She doubts herself, and everything that she's believed in for years. I told her the other night that I thought Jesus was knocking at her door, and she was not going to be able to keep him out, but . . . well, she's still looking for the truth. It isn't easy for her. Perhaps I'm not the right person to help

55

her.'

Toby felt sick with disappointment.

'Here,' said the doc, 'grab a tea-towel and make your-self useful. She didn't want you two to know, because she thought you might put pressure on her. I said you had a right to know, but she didn't agree about that, either.'

'It would be perfect,' said Toby.

'Look, even if she did accept Jesus into her life, and agreed to marry me, it might not be much fun for her, me being a doctor and liable to be called out all hours and come home tired and not fit to live with. I can see that, even if you can't.'

'I think it would be wonderful. I want to be a doctor myself one day.'

'Do you?' The doc gave Toby one of his penetrating looks. 'Now that is good news, the best I've heard for months. You'll have to work hard, though. All the sciences.'

'I will. I am. And I'll start praying for her, too.'

They talked about other things while they finished the washing up. The doc said he'd write Toby out a prescription, but the phone rang, and while the doc answered it, Toby found himself looking at a framed poem that hung on the wall.

Imagine you are sitting on the beach:
On your right stands a coconut palm.
You look at it carefully.
There are many nice green coconuts under it.

You wish to take one – because
It is clean,
It is pure,
It is good for you.

It costs nothing,
It is easy to carry,
It tastes good.

Jesus is like that coconut;
Offer him to others,
For the good of this world.

Toby thought that was a wonderful way of putting it. Trust the doc to know such a good poem.

The doc came off the phone, and said he'd got to rush out. He signed the prescription, and saw Toby to the door. It was getting lighter at nights. Starlings were swooping and chattering in the trees in the square.

Toby went out into the dusk. It felt like leaving paradise.

7

'You heard the fuzz raided the arcade?'

'I was there,' boasted Red. 'We saw it all, didn't we, Skinny?'

'Closed the Den, did they?'

'Nar. It's open again today. They didn't find nothing.'

'I heard they was looking for stolen tellies.'

'Who told you that?'

'Just heard it around. Tellies and videos and stereos and that. The fuzz thought 'Honest Joe' was fencing the stuff stolen from around the shopping centre.'

'Why pick on him? Harrassment, The Warden said. She says we gotta stop the fuzz thinking they can just walk in on anyone and close them down. She's gotta point, there.'

Toby hung around the edge of the group, kicking at a pebble and trying not to listen. His win at the arcade was a sore spot in his mind that he'd prefer not to touch. Luckily everyone seemed to think he'd lost all his winnings, since. Even Nikki thought that.

Toby couldn't come up with a single pleasant thing to think about. He couldn't think about home without worrying about the impending move. He couldn't think about his mum without worrying about whether she was going to turn her back on Jesus and move in with Jeff. It was even worse thinking about the doc, because now Toby knew that the doc really cared for his mum and for all of them.

At first he'd imagined he'd be all right if he could only get hold of a video, but even that consolation had gone. He might as well not have won the money, for all the good it had done him. Worse, he thought the others had been encouraged to spend more time on the machines because Toby had won.

He saw Fats across the playground. Fats was with Brains and Tooley and some of the other black players from the football team. Fats was looking across at Toby.

Toby turned his back on Fats, and listened to Skinny.

'I've got this feeling that I'm gonna win today. A black cat crossed the road this morning in front of me, on my way to school. I scrounged some money from Mum, and I'm going straight to the arcade after school.'

Red said, 'My mum said if I went there again, she'd give me what for. I don't know what I'm going to do. I've just got to get back in there. Mum found out I'd been spending me dinner money on the machines. Well, I couldn't help wanting more to eat in the evenings, could I? Mad with hunger, I was.'

Someone said, 'Well, I'm not going again. I lost all my pocket money, two weeks running and I'm saving up for a new skateboard.'

'You're just unlucky,' jeered Skinny. 'You gotta have a system, and you gotta have a lucky hand. Like Toby. You shoulda seen the money pouring out of the machine when he hit the jackpot!'

'Yeah, but he lost it all again, din't he?'

'He needn't have,' argued Skinny. 'He coulda put some money away, and played with the rest till he won again.'

The bell went and in the rush to get indoors, Toby was pushed to the floor. When he got up, his shirt was out of his trousers, and his pockets felt light. His belongings were on the floor – minus his dinner money.

That's all I need, thought Toby. Now we're stealing from one another, and the money won't go on food, but on the machines. He felt angry and sore because he thought it was Red who'd pushed him to the ground. Not that he could prove it.

He didn't want to believe a friend could do that to him.

No, it couldn't be Red. At lunchtime, he told Red and Skinny that he'd lost his dinner money and could they lend him some, so's he could get some chips for lunch. Toby watched Red's face but he didn't look self-conscious. That was a relief. At least it wasn't his own friend who'd robbed him.

Even so, getting a loan from them was like pulling teeth. Toby wanted to remind them that they both owed him plenty from the time when he'd hit the jackpot. He could see they remembered it, too, but didn't want to think about it.

Finally Skinny came up with fifty pence, and said that made them quits, didn't it? Well, it didn't, not by a long chalk, but Toby had to take it, and pretend that it did. He'd keep his dinner money in an inside pocket in future.

Nikki was going swimming after school, so Toby loitered, going home. He didn't want to go into the arcade. Ideally he'd have liked to go and see the doc, but he couldn't keep bothering the doc when he was so busy. No-one had any time to spend with him nowadays.

Toby told himself he was getting an attack of self-pity, and to do something about it, quickly. Who else could he go and see? Well, there was Mr Gaunt. Toby and Fats had helped out when Mr Gaunt had been confined to his bed some time back. Maybe he'd be willing to chat for a while.

Mr Gaunt had been churchwarden and then caretaker of the bombed church, and he still held the keys to the tower. They called him The Cheshire Cat. Usually his mouth turned down at the corners and you wouldn't think he'd ever had a pleasant thought in his life. But when he smiled, it was the biggest grin you ever saw, and you could tell he was a lovely person, inside.

Mr Gaunt was pottering about in a tiny lean-to greenhouse at the back of his terraced house. He was pricking out begonia seedlings, surrounded by the fragrance of half-grown tomato plants. Toby offered to help. He had clever fingers and Mr Gaunt said he could, if he were careful.

'They're getting on with the new church building,' said Mr Gaunt. 'I never thought I'd live to see it. I go past the site twice a day, and each time there's something new. I reckon they've just about dug out all the old foundations, now.'

'I miss being able to play on the Wasteland.'

'You'll have your chance later. They're getting someone from the Parks Department to make the garden and play area. It'll be right under your window.'

'We won't be there. We're being turned out.'

'What? Speak up, lad. I'm not deaf, but I can't hear if you mumble. You lads are all the same. Never been taught to speak properly.'

'I said, We've been given notice to quit!'

'No need to shout. Well, well. I don't know what they want to pull down perfectly good buildings for. We were lucky, our block's being modernised, instead of pulled down. I don't think I'd have survived being transplanted, at my age. Don't look so bad. They'll find you something else. What's this I hear about your mother starting a drop-in centre? We shan't know ourselves, soon.'

'It's not only that,' said Toby. 'I didn't think I'd mind not being able to get into the church tower, but I do. It was quiet up there, and well, it made you feel good. Mr

Gaunt, where do you go to church?'

'We get on the tube, the missus and me, and we go up to a big church in the City for a mid-week service. She likes the music there. Where do you go now, then?'

Toby didn't want to tell the truth, which was 'nowhere', so he tried for a diversion.

'You saw the mobile caff? That woman's got herself an old tin helmet, and says to call her "Warden".'

'Impudence! I'll give her "Warden." Plain Betty Jane Clark, that's who she is.'

'She says she's lived around here for ever.'

'So she has. You get all sorts.'

'And her son, who calls himself "Honest Joe"?'

'The only honest thing about him is . . . now, now, lad. You'll have me gossiping in a minute, and I don't hold with gossip.'

''Tisn't gossip, exactly. It's needing to know. A lot of my friends, Nikki too, they go into the arcade. The police raided it, and someone said they were looking for stolen goods. Mum and the doc, they said not to go into the arcade, but we all do.'

'You as well? I thought you'd more sense.'

'Maybe I have, now. But I did go.' It was a great relief to be able to talk about it. 'Only, Nikki still does, and so do Red and Skinny and a lot of the others. It's exciting. And some people have won a bit here and there. I can't see why it's wrong.'

'It's like this,' said Mr Gaunt. 'The highlight of the year for my father was a day trip to the Derby and a small bet on the horses. Never more than one bet, and never more than sixpence. My mother used to say, A little of what you fancy does you good.

'But my uncle, he was different. He took it too far. He had to bet on every race meeting, and it wasn't just sixpences he'd bet. No, it was every penny he could lay his hands on. Now sometimes he'd win, but more often than not he'd lose. It got so's he had to sell his good clothes, and then he lost his job and couldn't get another because people knew he couldn't be relied on. Casual labour, that was all he could manage for the last fifteen, twenty years of his life. The excitement of gambling took him over, see.'

Toby thought of his friends, unable to talk of anything else.

'She used to quote St Paul at us. That was in the old days, before they had these new-fangled versions.' The old man lifted a claw-like hand, and half-closed his eyes to remember the words. ' "All things are lawful for me, but I will not be brought under the power of any." Now how would you put that, young Toby?'

' "It's all right, so long as it doesn't take you over?" '

'Some things can get such a hold on you, that you can't break the habit. That's what happened to my uncle, and I reckon that's what could happen to your friends at the arcade. Instead of being in control – like my old dad – it could take them over, like it did my uncle. One man's meat is another man's poison. Does that answer your question?'

'Yes,' said Toby. 'Thanks.'

Running home, he thought he saw Red waiting for him on the other side of the road, in the doorway of the Webbs' flat. A bus passed between them, and by the time it had passed, the doorway was empty. Toby darted through the traffic, fumbling for his key.

But the door was ajar, and there were bright new gouges in the wood of the door-frame. He stared at the half-open door, feeling a cold shiver go down his back.

On the stairs was a scarf of his mum's. It looked as if she'd dropped it on her way out. Only Toby knew that she'd left before him that morning, and there hadn't been a scarf on the stairs then.

Nikki came panting up. 'What's up? You look as if

you've seen the Horror of Paradise Row.'
    'I think we've been burgled!'

8

The police had come and gone. Toby and Nikki sat limply at the kitchen table, trying to eat their supper. Their mum sat smoking at the end of the table, with a cup of coffee before her.

Nikki sniffed. She'd lost the silver locket she'd got from the doc last birthday.

Kate Webb flicked ash from her cigarette, and kept her eyes on the table. Her portable typewriter had gone. Luckily she'd been wearing her engagement ring and her mother's silver brooch, but her new jet earrings had gone.

The telly had gone. Toby knew that was what they were all going to miss the most. It was time for *Neighbours*, and they couldn't watch it. They couldn't watch anything. Toby's room was undisturbed.

Kate said, 'Well, this won't get the baby his bath . . .' and continued to sit there, staring at nothing.

Toby said, 'How much would a good second-hand telly cost?'

'Black and white? Not much. We'll see what we can do at the end of the month. Rent one, perhaps. Only, there's your school trip to France to pay for.'

They hadn't any insurance. Toby knew his mum was kicking herself for letting the insurance lapse, but things had been so tight, she hadn't thought it as important as getting them new shoes and keeping their old car going.

The policeman had made it clear he didn't expect they'd see their things again. There'd been a lot of burglaries in the neighbourhood, and nothing had been recovered so far. He asked Kate to keep a look out for their things turning up in pubs, or flea-markets. He said the police would circulate the description of their stuff, but being, well, not very expensive, it probably wouldn't even get as far as the second-hand shops.

They drifted into the front room out of habit. The shelf was empty where the telly had stood. The twins averted their eyes.

The burglar had pushed Kate's papers onto the floor, probably while trying to get the portable typewriter into its case. It wasn't a new machine, but it was solid and everything worked except the tab. Kate began to pick up the papers. She'd been doing a report for work, drafting it on the typewriter.

Toby said, 'How will you manage all your reports and letters without a typewriter, mum?'

'I'll have to borrow one, or do them at the office. I'll manage, somehow.'

Nikki began to sniffle. 'I really liked that locket!'

'Oh!' cried Kate, and Toby could hear the pain in her voice. 'This awful place! I can't get out of here quick enough!'

Toby went up to his room, and shut the door. It hadn't looked as if the burglar had got as far as this, but he needed to check his secret hiding places. It was all right, the money was still there.

He sat down on the bed and thought about Red.

As Toby had come in sight of their front door, he'd seen someone dart away from it. He suspected that that someone was Red, but he couldn't be sure. When the police had asked if Toby had seen anybody, he'd hesitated, and then said 'no'.

He really couldn't be sure. It had been so quick, that

glimpse of . . . whoever it was. It might have been Red, or it might have been one of two or three other ginger-headed kids from school. If it was Red, he might have had a legitimate reason for being there, like trying to call on Toby and banging on the door, expecting him to be home. If the door had already been broken open, any push on it would have made it fall in, and then Red would have realised something was wrong and scarpered, just as Toby crossed the road.

It was like a dragging pain, suspecting one of your best mates for a thing like that. Because if it was Red, then it wasn't just a burglary, but also a betrayal. Red knew the Webbs were badly off. He knew they hadn't got a colour telly, or a video or anything like that. He couldn't have helped rob his own friends, could he?

Toby reached for his inhaler. Should he tell the police what he'd seen? Or should he go round and have it out with Red? Yes, that was what he'd do. One look, and he was sure he'd know. The more he thought about it, the more impossible it seemed that Red would have done it. Toby was glad he hadn't told the police.

But what was he to do about the money? He could give it to his mum, and she could replace the typewriter with it, because she really needed a typewriter for her work.

He sat on his bed, holding the money, feeling its weight and warmth within his hand. There was a lot of money there. He'd checked in the window of the second-hand shop, and he could get a second-hand video for just under a hundred pounds. Of course, he hadn't got a hundred yet, but with another good run of luck . . .

Why should he give his money to his mum? Nikki had had her share of his money, and if she'd been careful like him, she'd now have something to put towards a new typewriter, but look what she'd done with it! Lost it. Just like the others. They'd been stupid, but he'd been clever, and hung on to his. It was his by rights and he had a right to spend it as he wished.

On the other hand, a video wasn't any use unless you had a telly first. It was a problem. He'd have to think about it. He put the money back into its hiding place and went out to look for Red.

Mr Red was the foreman at a local builder's, and doing very well, thank you. The family had a nice new car to drive around in nowadays, and Toby could see the flicker of a giant colour telly through the net curtains at the front window.

Mrs Red came to the door, a portable telephone clamped to one ear. She said, 'Hold on a mo . . . no, Toby, he's not in. It's football tonight, isn't it? He won't be back till late.'

She resumed her conversation and shut the door. Toby rubbed the back of his neck. It wasn't football that night, and anyway, Red wasn't in any of the football teams.

It was more than a bit odd that Red's mum didn't know where he was, but if he wasn't home, he'd be at the arcade. He was crazy about those games machines.

Toby had read about feelings of Impending Doom. It felt like that now, as if a great black thunder cloud was about to burst over his head.

He looked in the arcade and there was Red, hair standing up all over his head, frenziedly working one of the machines. He was alone. No Skinny. No-one else Toby knew.

Except, in the far back corner, there was a scuffed school bag with a small yellow duck stuck on it. Nikki was also playing the machines.

Toby hovered outside, watching.

Red was totally absorbed. His time was up, and he fed another token into the machine without wasting a second. Nikki was also absorbed. She hadn't turned round, hadn't seen him. Neither had Red.

Red stood back from his machine and felt in all his pockets. Zilch. He stood there, chewing on his lip, and then went to the booth and asked Honest Joe for something. More tokens? Credit?

Joe shook his head, but Red didn't leave. He stuck in there, mooching around. After a while, Joe gave Red a broom, and he started sweeping up the fag ends and bits of paper and empty Coke tins that littered the floor.

Toby didn't know why he went on watching. He could have gone in and asked Red straight out what he'd been doing since he left school. But he didn't. Nikki finished playing the machine. She also went up to the booth, and had a short conversation with Joe. Then she came out, looking angry.

She walked right past Toby without seeing him. He was going to say Hi, but she suddenly spurted off through the traffic.

He turned back to the arcade. Red was playing the machines again. Toby gaped. How could he have got more money? Ah, perhaps he'd been paid for cleaning the place up, in tokens.

Well, that was all right, wasn't it?

Toby crossed the road and went to peer through one of the 'windows' in the hoardings, looking down into the great hole where the Wasteland had been.

Someone put a hand on his shoulder, but Toby didn't even jump. He knew that touch.

'Hi,' he said.

'Hi,' said the doc. 'Just passing. I have to have a look, too, every time I pass. Getting on well, aren't they? These builders have got a good reputation, usually complete on time. Look at the materials they're delivering. All good stuff. They're starting on the foundations next week, I hear. That'll be a day to remember. At least this church will be soundly built, and won't fall down at the first spot of rain.'

Toby wasn't sure what the doc was talking about, and it showed.

'It's a parable,' explained the doc. 'The wise man builds his house upon rock, which is faith in Jesus. That way his house withstands storm and tempest, and whatever the world can throw at him. The foolish man builds upon sand, which melts away when bad weather comes. Got it? This church should see us out.'

'Unlike our flat,' said Toby. The street was getting a shabby look. Well, it had always been shabby, but now it was getting worse. The newsagents next door to them had closed, and so had several other shops in the block.

'Yes, it's a pity. Good enough housing, in its way, and could have been renovated. But the developers say they can get more people on the site, by pulling the houses down and building flats.'

'Flats!' said Toby in disgust.

'Some flats are all right. How's your mother? And Nikki?'

'We got burgled.'

The doc looked shocked. He asked for details, and said he'd call in later, see what he could do. Toby wanted to ask if he could go on his rounds with the doc, but he didn't think that would be allowed, so he smiled and waved as the doc drove off. He looked across at the arcade. Red wasn't there any more, so Toby went round to Red's house again.

Red came to the door, looking sullen. When he saw Toby, he hesitated. Toby had a flash of insight. He thought, 'Red knows about the robbery, and he's going to lie.'

Toby said, 'Red, I've got a problem. We've just been . . .'

'Stuff your problem. I've got enough problems of my own.'

Toby couldn't believe what he was hearing. Red hadn't ever been rude to him like that before.

'Who's that?' shouted his mum from inside.

'No-one!' Red shouted back. He came out onto the step. 'Listen, I've had enough of you, hanging around and wanting to borrow money. I ain't got no money for you. Have you got that straight?'

'That wasn't what I came for,' said Toby, beginning to get angry. 'We've been burgled and when I was coming home, I thought I saw you leaving our . . .'

'Well, you didn't. And if you go around telling people that you did, then you're nothing but a rotten liar, and I shall tell them so, and what's more, they'll believe me, so you'd better shut up and get lost, right?'

'There's no need to be like that!' said Toby. 'I didn't tell the police I saw you, because I hoped I was wrong . . .'

'So you was! I wasn't there, and I didn't have nothing to do with it. You get out and stay out, and don't come round again, or I'll see you get something to make you keep quiet.'

'Such as?'

'I've got friends. Not your type of friend, but really good friends, who know how to look after me. They don't like your sort, any more'n I do. Everyone's talking about you, Toby Webb. What a wimp, that's what they say! The most unpopular boy in the school! We can't wait till you leave for your posh school.'

'But I'm not . . .'

'Oh yes, you are. You'd better make up your mind to that, and quick. Or your mind will be made up for you. Get it?'

Red went back inside his house, and banged the door in Toby's face.

9

Toby was angry enough to kick the door in. Then he thought, Was that really what people thought about him?

No, it just wasn't true. Red had lied, because he was guilty and wanted to put Toby down.

That wasn't a good thought, either.

Toby set off for home. His chest was so tight he could hardly squeeze the breath in and out of his lungs.

He got out his inhaler and puffed away. It didn't help much. He was so angry, he simply couldn't control his breathing. He wanted to hit Red, and go on hitting him till Red took back what he'd said.

He wanted to go to the police station, and tell them that Red had been involved in the burglary at their flat.

He wanted to howl because he'd lost a friend.

Toby was convinced now that Red had been implicated in the burglary. On the surface it didn't make sense, because Red's family had lots of money, at least compared to everyone else around. But if Red had got tied up with Honest Joe at the Thieves Den, then maybe . . . Toby thought, am I really the most unpopular boy in the school? Do they really think I'm a wimp?

Perhaps I am, and . . .

No, I'm not. It's just the asthma, and being a bit different perhaps, and Jeff going on about a posh school . . .

'Whoa!'

Toby rebounded off something large and hard. He staggered back, and a huge hand and arm caught hold of his shoulder to steady him. 'Don't you look where you're going no more?'

Fats was grinning down at him. Toby tried to grin back, but it wasn't much of an effort.

'I heard about the burglary,' said Fats. 'That's really bad, man. Did you lose much?'

'The telly, mum's typewriter, some bits of jewellery.'

'Hey, hey,' said Fats. 'I am sorry.'

Suddenly Toby felt like singing because Fats was looking down at him with affection. Fats obviously didn't think he was a wimp.

'Where you off to, then?' said Fats. 'We got off practice early. I've been taken on by the team, told to report this Saturday for a match. Only as reserve, but it's a start, ain't it? Wondered if you'd like to come and watch me make a fool of myself.'

'Yes, I would,' said Toby, and meant it. 'When and where?'

'School, half ten. I thought of asking Red and Skinny and the rest, but then I thought I might not get a chance to play, only being reserve and that. But I'd really like it, if you came.'

'I'll be there,' said Toby, feeling humble but also very happy. 'I wouldn't miss it for anything.'

'Sorry I haven't been able to come out with you and the camera. It's been on me mind, but somehow . . . it mops up your time, this football.'

'That's all right. Perhaps we can do it in the summer months, when football's stopped.'

'Someone said you might be sent away to school.'

'Jeff wants to get rid of us. Get Mum to himself. Me and Nikki, we're not into posh schools.' Toby looked at Fats, to see if he'd come out with that wimp label. But he didn't.

Fats nodded, and that was all.

He accepts me as I am, thought Toby. He felt ashamed of how nearly he'd nearly lost his good friend, and that shame prompted him to action.

'Listen, Fats. I wanted to say I was stupid about your joining the football team. And I've missed you.'

'Sure. I missed you, too.'

They studied the traffic lights, careful not to let the conversation get too heavy.

Toby said, 'What's more, I ought to have taken you up on that invitation, to go with you and your family to your church. I didn't realise how much I'd miss it, when we couldn't even get into our church tower, or talk to the doc about things that bothered us.'

'Yeah,' said Fats. 'Odd, innit? We kinda took it for granted. I know the doc said it was the people that was the church, and not the building, but somehow, it makes it a whole lot easier when you meet up regularly with mates who are also into Jesus. I always stop and look, every time I pass the church site. Some of my mates from the football team, they caught me looking, and we got talking about it, and do you know, they said – well, one of them did – they might come when the church is opened up again.'

Toby thought how much nicer Fats was than anyone else he knew, except perhaps the doc. Fats was so sure of his love for Jesus, and of Jesus' love for him, that he could even talk to his team-mates about the church. Perhaps that casual conversation with Fats would mean another boy being brought into the warmth of Jesus' love.

By contrast, Toby felt grey and useless. What had he done for Jesus of late? Nothing. Worse, he'd helped lead some of his friends down a very dicey alley.

They'd reached Toby's front door. The newsagents was shut and forlorn, and the windows of the flat above

were blank. Knowing that neighbourhood, tomorrow or
the next day there'd be a brick through those windows.

'Will you come up?' said Toby.

'Can't. Got to babysit.'

'Well, see you tomorrow.'

'And Saturday at the match?'

'And Sunday, at your church. Right?'

'Right.'

Fats did get to play in the match on Saturday morning,
and though he didn't score five goals and rescue the team
single-handed from defeat, he certainly earned his place.
He didn't get mad when a member of the opposite team
brought him down with a foul, either. Toby, well
wrapped up against the bitter wind, hopped up and
down, and cheered himself hoarse. Their team won with
a respectable three to one goals, and Fats' grin widened
to split his face in half.

'Whatja think? Ain't Tooley and Brains got the game
sussed? Didja hear them say I could play again next
season? And they want me to keep on practising with
them, coupla nights a week, through Easter . . .'

Fats couldn't stop talking.

'Hey, Tooley!' said Fats, bringing one of his mates
over to talk to Toby. 'This is my mate, Toby, that I was
telling you about. You know, about the new church and
all that. Toby's the one you oughta talk to, if you want
to come along some time.'

'Sure!' Toby got his hand pulped by yet another big
black lad.

'And this is Brains – called Brains 'cos he ain't got
any, except for football.'

'Wow!' said Toby, 'Do you know how to get that ball
to do what you want, or do you!'

'Practice, man!' said Brains, also grinning. 'They say
I ain't got no brains, but I makes up for it with practice!'

'See you!' shouted Fats, waving to his team mates as he went off with Toby. 'Boy, oh boy! Was that unreal! I never thought I'd actually get to play with them this side of Christmas! And they all play fair, giving me a chance, covering my mistakes . . . Praise the Lord, allelujah!'

'Right on!' said Toby. In this mood you couldn't do anything but nod and agree with Fats, because he'd babble on till he'd talked himself down from the clouds. Toby didn't mind. He didn't mind anything, so long as things were all right between him and Fats again. And tomorrow he'd be going to church with Fats, and maybe he'd feel more at peace with himself after that.

Toby didn't expect any particular hassle from his mum about going to church, and in fact there wasn't any, not like there had been in the past. She seemed a bit surprised but not annoyed, though she did say that Jeff was coming to lunch and Toby shouldn't be late because Jeff wanted to talk about his new school.

It was a long walk to the church where Mrs Fats took her family, but Toby didn't mind. He felt a sense of purpose as they walked along. He was even sorry for the kids who hung around street corners or got up to mischief out of boredom on Sunday mornings.

The church wasn't very big or very old, and it didn't have that cold stiffness that Toby associated with churches you went to look at, rather than worship in. Everyone greeted everyone else as they walked in, and Toby was smiled at, and had his hand shaken so many times he felt really welcome.

The service was something else. It was Palm Sunday, and everyone was remembering how Jesus had been given a sort of Wall-Street-ticker-tape welcome into Jerusalem, only to be betrayed by one of his closest friends to torture and death. It was hallelujah with an aching heart, knowing what was to come.

It was remembering how Jesus had asked his friends to sit up with him while he went through the last great temptation . . . and having them fail him again and again.

It really broke Toby up.

'Whatsa matter?' hissed Fats, under cover of the hymn singing.

'Tell you after,' whispered Toby. It was no good, he couldn't keep it to himself any longer. Toby didn't like to think of the way Fats would take it. Fats was his only real friend, apart from the doc, and the doc wasn't readily available, was he?

Only just then an astonishing thing happened.

The door at the back opened, and the doc slipped into the church. He was evidently well known there, for a man smiled, shook his hand, and made room for him in his pew. The doc picked up the tune, and joined in the hymn singing. Then he saw Toby looking at him. He grinned and waggled his eyebrows.

Toby looked up at the cross at the front of the church and it was just as if Jesus had spoken to him. 'OK, Toby. You say you're sorry for what you've been up to. Prove it. I've made the opportunity for you to tell your two best friends all about it, so get on with it. And remember, I'm always here. It wasn't I who deserted you, but you who turned away from me . . .'

Toby looked at Fats, and he looked at the doc. They were singing away with clear consciences, happy at being in the presence of Jesus, among his friends . . . doing their best to follow in his ways.

Toby felt himself to be a very grubby little soul by contrast. He shrank from telling them what he'd been up to. What if they turned from him in disgust, as they had every right to do?

Toby didn't know how he could bear it.

10

After the service, practically everyone moved into the adjoining church hall for coffee and a chat. Toby found himself hoping that the doc would have to rush off somewhere, which would postpone Toby's confession. The doc didn't. He even came up to Toby and Fats, and said, 'Let's find a corner where we can talk. How are you getting on, Fats? I haven't seen you for ages.'

Toby couldn't wriggle out of it any longer. He felt as if Jesus' eyes were on him, prodding him into action. Fats started telling the doc about the football team, and about how Brains and Tooley had shown some interest in the rebuilding of the church. All the while Toby kept quiet. He was hoping the doc's bleeper would go off and take him away.

It didn't. No-one came up to interrupt them, either, although that was what usually happened when the doc was in company.

'Right,' said the doc. 'So what's Toby been up to?'

Toby felt as if his tongue had grown fur. 'You won't like it, but I've got to tell you, I suppose.'

'Uh-huh!' said the doc. 'I did wonder . . .'

'It's my fault!' said Fats. 'I knew something was wrong, but I let it go on . . .'

'No, it was my fault,' said Toby. 'I did something completely stupid, and it wasn't so very wrong in itself, but it helped make some of my friends go wrong, and then I stopped but they didn't and now it's got serious, and I don't know what to do about it. And what's more, it set up a barrier between myself and Fats . . .'

He told them what had happened, from the moment he went into the arcade against Fats' advice. He told them about his win, and how it had set up all sorts of problems with his friends and family, and about Nikki still going there, and Red's odd behaviour. Then, with some hesitation, he told them he'd seen Red – or maybe it wasn't him, but someone very like him – leaving their doorway after the burglary.

The doc hit his knee. 'I blame myself. I knew what had happened before, but it was all so long ago, and I thought I was over-reacting. Then there was the move . . . no, I've no excuse. I ought to have done something.'

'What?' said Toby. 'You couldn't have stopped me going in there, and once I'd been unlucky enough to win . . .'

'You and Nikki wanted to know about "Honest Joe" and his mother, and I wouldn't tell you. I thought it would be taking away a man's reputation when he was trying to go straight. I thought he'd stopped all that, but . . . the damage they've done!'

Fats said, 'Me mum told me they were bad news, and especially bad to children. I thought they was rigging the machines not to pay out properly. There's more?'

'Yes,' said the doc. 'I'm afraid so. Some years ago they were convicted of receiving stolen goods. If that were all, it would be bad enough, but it came out at the trial that they'd been encouraging youngsters to get into debt through playing the machines. When the kids couldn't pay their debts, or their parents couldn't do it for them, "Honest Joe" and his mother sent the kids out to steal. The idea was that the kids would work off their debts that way, but what really happened was that they just got deeper in.

'Worse, one of the kids tried to break away, and he was beaten up, and that frightened the rest into keeping quiet. When it came to trial, the Clarks went to jail and two of the older kids were sent to special schools.'

'You mean, you think that Red . . . ?'

'. . . and Nikki!'

'I think,' said the doc, 'that I'd better come back home with you, Toby, and have a chat to Nikki, and to your mum.'

Toby felt feverish. 'But if Nikki's got into debt, we can't possibly pay . . . unless . . .' He remembered the money he'd still got hidden away. 'OK,' he said. 'I see what I've got to do. I've got to use my winnings to get Nikki clear.'

'But what about Red?' said Fats, looking troubled.

The doc said, 'I happen to know he's off school, not feeling too clever. His mum's been into the surgery and asked if I'd drop in on him. She'd tried to get him in to see me, but he refused. I hope the Clarks haven't been working on him to . . . well, I'll see him today, after I've spoken to Nikki.'

Walking home, Toby felt a great sense of release. He'd told his friends everything, and they hadn't turned away from him.

Jesus hadn't turned away from his friends, even though they'd let him down something chronic. It was Toby who'd turned away from Jesus, not the other way round. Jesus had always been there, but Toby had muddied his channel of communication by letting the bad things take him over.

Well, Mr Gaunt had been right about the arcade. It had let loose greed and envy in the community. It had given the neighbourhood an excitement . . . but it had been the wrong sort of excitement. Watching the football the previous day had been much more exciting and hadn't cost Toby a penny.

They came to the building site, and parted from Mrs Fats and her family. Toby and the doc went on to the Webbs' flat.

Toby smelt cigarettes, as soon as they opened the front door. 'I forgot, Mum said Jeff's coming round. He wants to talk to us about going to his posh school.'

The doc went up the stairs and into the living-room. He said hello nicely to Kate, and politely to Jeff. Nikki ran straight to him and gave him a hug. Toby spotted that Nikki was on the verge of tears. He was angry with himself for not having realised Nikki was in trouble. He ought to have seen it and done something about it, but instead, he'd sat around saying 'There, There!' to himself.

When she saw the doc, Kate jumped to her feet and Toby wondered if she were going to rush to the doc and hug him, too. But she didn't. Her smile vanished, and suddenly she looked as if she might cry. Toby wanted to run to her and hug her. The doc must have had the same impulse, because he started across the room towards her . . . and then stopped himself. Kate sniffed, hard. She asked if anyone wanted some more coffee.

Toby offered to get the coffee, and the doc swept Nikki off into the kitchen, too. Toby went to the loo so the doc could talk to Nikki on his own, and when he got back, she had her head on his shoulder, and was crying. The doc had his arm round her.

The doc reached out a hand for Toby, and drew him in as well. That felt better.

'This silly girl . . .' said the doc.

'I know I ought not to have, but it was so easy at first, and that man said it didn't matter one bit, carrying over what I owed till the end of the week, but by that time it was more than my next week's pocket money, and . . . and . . .'

'How much do you owe?' said the doc, gently.

'Nearly twenty pounds!' said Nikki, gulping. 'I thought my luck must change, but it didn't, and I couldn't tell mum because we're always so short, and then there was the burglary, and they stole my little silver locket . . .'

Toby said, 'I'll settle the debt.'

'How?' said Nikki, trying to mop herself up.

'My winnings. I kept some back. Do we have to tell mum?'

'That's up to you,' said the doc, 'but I think you'll feel better if you do. If you're brave enough, you should tell everyone what happened. It might help some of your friends who've got into trouble in the same way.'

Nikki sniffed. 'Jan and Clare won't go again. Jan said she'd sooner drop the money down the drain.'

Toby said, 'What about Red? Nikki, I'm really worried about him. Do you know how he manages to keep playing every day?'

'Never thought about it,' said Nikki, going to the fridge and pouring herself a drink of milk. 'It is odd about Red, I suppose. He does some cleaning for Honest Joe and gets paid in tokens. Only . . .'

She was silent, thinking.

The doc said, 'Nikki, if you know anything that might help, I think you should tell us. Red may be in serious trouble.'

'Well, he's changed. Nowadays he bites your head off if you say anything to him. Jan says he's been bunking off school. She knows, because they live in the same road. He said it was because he was sleeping badly. Having nightmares. That's true, because his mum complained to her mum about Red's disturbing them, almost every night. His mum wanted him to see you about it, but Red wouldn't. He said he just needed to take things easy for a while.'

'Anything else?'

Nikki thought about it. 'Well . . . he runs errands for a couple of the big kids who hang around the arcade. Fetching chips and Coke, that sort of thing. Yet he seems almost, well, afraid of them. They're not very nice to him. They say things like, "Red's afraid of the dark, isn't he?" Or, "You want another dose of . . ." Something. I wasn't really listening. I didn't think it was important.'

'I think,' said the doc, 'that these nightmares need investigating. I'll go and see Red right away.'

'Nikki! Toby!' It was their mum. 'What about Jeff's coffee?'

Nikki said, 'Bother. I'll get it. The Beard wants to talk to us about the school. Or rather, he wants to point out how good and kind he is, to send us there.'

The doc put his hand on her shoulder. 'Nikki, I want you to be clear in your mind about this. Are you being awkward about going to this school because you don't think it's a good idea, or because you don't get on with Jeff?'

She squirmed a bit. 'I hate the thought of having to live in his flat, and be polite to him all the time.'

'But what about the school?'

She pulled at a loose thread on his sweater. 'The school might be all right. I don't know. I'm settled here, and it's not so bad, and I've got friends and all. It would be different if . . . you know . . . if we belonged somewhere else.'

'And you, Toby?'

'I wouldn't like it, whatever happened. I suppose I could put up with it if things were different, if we were able to live with you, and you really felt I ought to give it a try. But there's Fats, and everything that goes on around here. I belong here now.'

'Roots,' said the doc, more to himself than to them.

'Yes.'

The doc promised to escort Nikki to pay her debt to Honest Joe, and left to see Red. The twins went into the living-room to confront the Beard.

The Beard excelled himself. He called them 'my dear Nikki', and 'my old son'. He said he had fixed up an interview for them with the Head of their new school. They would be shown around in the afternoon and take a test, just a formality, of course, but . . .

'What happens if we muck up the test?' asked Nikki.

The Beard gasped. Toby turned a laugh into a cough, and Nikki smiled.

'You wouldn't dare!' said their mother.

'Of course not,' said Nikki, looking innocent. 'Except accidentally on purpose we might. Some days I can't even spell my name, can I, Toby?'

'I can spell "Beard",' said Toby. 'It goes "e-r-r-o-r".'

Kate went bright red. 'Kids, I'll speak to you later!'

Toby turned to the Beard, whose mouth was hanging open. 'We're afraid we might let you down if you took us to this school of yours. Like, living round here, we don't 'arf use some bad language, and we do mucky things like picking our noses . . .'

'Some days,' added Nikki, 'we don't seem to be able to keep our clothes clean and tidy . . .'

'. . . and we have been known to be sick in the car . . .'

'You mean you'd deliberately throw away the best chance you're ever likely to . . . ?'

'To be shot out of your way so's you can concentrate on Mum? No thanks.'

'Why, you ungrateful . . . !'

'Right. We don't know why you bother with us.'

'I don't either,' said their mum. 'Out, kids! This instant! I'll speak to you later!'

'I'd better be going, too,' said Jeff. 'Look at the time!'

He went. Kate clenched her hands into fists, gave an angry scream, and disappeared into her own bedroom.

'Did we win that round, or did we?' asked Nikki.

'We did. But remember, it's not the first, but the last round that counts.'

11

Toby couldn't be sure when spring arrived. It certainly wasn't on the first official day of spring, because that was grey with rain and depression. It wasn't the day he first saw pale leaves struggling to unfurl on a sapling in the shopping centre, either.

Maybe it was the day they broke up for the Easter holidays, when he saw the fat red, white and blue hyacinths bulging out of Mr Gaunt's window box.

Toby was looking for Red at the time. Lots of people were. His mum said he'd gone to stay for a few days with a school-friend, down Southend way. Nikki said she'd heard Skinny knew something. But Skinny lived in the flats, and not 'Southend way'.

The arcade was packed. Groups of kids hung around the doors, waiting for someone to leave so they could get in. There'd been a couple of fights at the arcade, and more attention from the police.

Kate Webb said the neighbourhood was going downhill. There was hardly a shop left open around their way. The ghetto-blaster on the mobile café was turned on at half past six in the morning, and not turned off till long after Toby had fallen asleep at night. He'd learned to sleep through it, as he'd learned to disregard the sharper noises made by trucks and lorries and cement mixers on the site.

Toby peered through the 'window' in the hoarding,

to see how far the walls had risen on the foundations since the day before. The new building looked ridiculously small. When there had just been a large hole, the space had looked enormous, but it didn't seem possible to swing a cat in the new basement.

They were using breeze-blocks between steel girders to form the skeleton of the building, and clothing it with a red brick skin. The doc had told Toby that once they reached ground floor level, the outer framework would be quick to rise, until they reached the roof. Once the roof was on, they could take their time fitting out the building inside, putting in windows and doors and lifts and so on. But the basement was complicated, because they had to account for plumbing and water and electricity and all sorts of things that people took for granted. You had to get those right from the very beginning, or there'd be trouble.

'Imagine a building without any drains,' Fats had said, the other day. 'Recipe for disaster.'

Toby had agreed. 'Yeah, that would be a house built on sand, wouldn't it?'

They looked across at the arcade. 'That's built on sand,' said Fats. 'It's built on excitement, and greed. False values.'

'Atishoo, atishoo, all fall down,' said Toby. 'But what could make it fall down?'

Fats shrugged. 'Mum says there was another police raid there, our last day at school. They didn't find nothing. We just gotta go on praying about it, I guess. Well, see ya.' He waved and went off.

Toby turned away from the 'window' and looked around for Nikki, who had promised to meet him at four. The doc had been so busy that he'd not been able to take her to pay off her debt at the Den, so Toby had said he'd go with her instead.

She came at last, dragging her swimming things in a

plastic bag along the pavement behind her.

'Do we have to?' she asked.

'Yes,' said Toby. 'You know we do.'

'We couldn't wait till the doc's free?'

'And risk Honest Joe trying to charge you interest?'

'Ouch! Oh, all right. But look at the place! We'll never get in. There's far too many people there.'

'We'll manage.'

Toby felt the roll of coins wrapped in paper at the bottom of his pocket. He wasn't carrying it in his bag, for fear it might be pinched.

They crossed the road and wriggled their way into the Den. There was too much cigarette smoke in the air for Toby's liking, but he persevered. Nikki was following him, and not leading the way like she usually did. He couldn't see Red, or Skinny, or anyone he knew.

He got trodden on by a couple of large young men, and he thought it was probably more on purpose than by accident. That made him angry, and he pushed his way through to the back of the shop. A grille had been installed in the corner, to protect Honest Joe and his takings from casual theft.

The big man was there, smoking, drinking from a can, with his beer belly overhanging the counter. He was a formidable size, and made Toby feel even smaller than usual.

'Hello, shrimp,' said Honest Joe. 'How many tokens do you want this time?'

'I've come to pay off my sister's debt.'

'Well, that's between her and me, eh? So how many tokens do you want to buy?'

'None.' Toby brought out his roll of coins. 'I'd like a receipt for it, please, saying she's paid in full.'

Honest Joe gave a full-throated roar of laughter. At least, it was meant to be laughter, but it didn't sound as if he were really amused.

Nikki squirmed in front of Toby. 'He's right. I would like a receipt.'

'What?' He put his great ham-like fists on the counter, and brought his head down to look at her. 'Why, if it isn't my little chickadee! You'll have to wait a while to get at your favourite machine, darling. Why don't you come back early tomorrow, instead? All the time in the world to play the machines in the holidays.'

'I don't want to play any more. I just want to pay what I owe.'

Toby laid the roll of money on the counter, but kept his hand on it. 'There's twenty pounds there. I believe she owes you nineteen pounds something.'

'She owes me more than that,' Honest Joe said, turning his smile off. He laid his own hand over Toby's, and the roll of coins disappeared. 'But I'll take this to be going on with.'

'Count it, please,' said Toby, 'and let me have a receipt.'

'Another time. Now, move on. There's others waiting.'

'I'm not going till I've got a receipt,' said Toby.

'Get out while I'm still in a good mood! There's a queue behind you, waiting to be served.'

'If you try to throw me out without a receipt, then I'll go straight to the police and . . .'

'You . . . !' The big man checked himself. 'You know what, Shrimp, you're making yourself very unpopular around here. Very unpopular indeed. You're not liked. And people that aren't liked don't last long around here. Get it?'

'I still want that receipt,' said Toby, his back stiff.

The big man said something under his breath, but a couple of lads in the queue behind Toby said, 'Oh, give the boy his bit of paper,' so he did.

Toby checked that it cancelled Nikki's debt and put

it carefully away in an inside pocket before leaving the counter. He didn't trust anyone there.

Once outside, Nikki recovered enough to try to joke about it. 'So you're "not liked" around here, are you? "Shrimp", eh?'

Toby shrugged. He supposed he'd start growing some day. He wished it was sooner rather than later, though. He was getting tired of being called 'Tich', and 'Shrimp'.

'Here's your receipt. Just don't lose it.'

'Toby, what he said . . . do you think he meant it?'

Toby shrugged again. 'So I take care not to walk down dark alleys if he's around. I'm going over to see Skinny. Want to come?'

Nikki dumped her swimming things at home and they went up the walkways and along the balcony to the fourth floor flat where Skinny lived. It was windy up there, but it felt cleaner than down in the street.

Toby leaned over the balcony and saw trees flowering in tiny garden patches below. Their block, next to the building site, looked derelict. For the first time he wished they'd moved as soon as they'd been given notice. Perhaps it wouldn't be so bad, living up in the flats. But so far Kate hadn't been offered anything fit to move into. Now and then she still mentioned that they might move in with Jeff, but she didn't talk about it as much as she used to. Toby was praying hard that some day soon her mind would clear out all its doubts, and she'd accept the love of Jesus . . . and the doc.

Skinny answered the door. The telly was on, and his mum was out, so Toby and Nikki went in.

'No, I ain't seen Red. Not since long before school broke up, maybe ten days ago. Caught him in the playground, thought he was crying, but he said he wasn't. Just caught his knee on something, he said. He looked awful, bags under eyes and that. Said he were having nightmares. About being shut up in the dark, and not able to breathe. Told me if I weren't careful, I'd get them, too. I asked him what he meant, and he gave me a real funny look. Haven't seen him since.'

'We heard he'd been working in the arcade.'

'Yeah. I heard that, too, but I've stopped going.'

His eyes slid to Nikki. Toby thought, he knows Nikki got into debt at the Den, but he doesn't want to give her away, not even to me.

Nikki said, 'It's all right, Skinny. Toby knows. My debt's been paid off, and I'm not going back, either.'

Toby said, 'Do you think the machines are rigged?'

'Well, I got talking to a guy there, used to be a friend of me brother's. This chap said all fruit machines were rigged, but some more so than others. He offered to show me how to get the machines to pay out, but then old Joe come up and told us what he'd do to us if we tampered with his precious machines, and I split, sharpish. It wasn't worth it.'

Toby was curious. 'What did he say he'd do to you?'

Skinny grimaced. 'It wasn't so much what he said as the way he said it, if you know what I mean. I believed him. He's bad news.'

'Do you think he did something bad to Red, and that that's why Red's scarpered?'

'His mum says he's in Southend, having a break with a friend.'

They looked at one another, and shrugged. If he was in Southend, then he was all right. Until he returned.

Kate Webb was cooking dinner when they got back. 'The doc's invited us to go to the fun fair with him at the weekend. I said we'd go.'

'What, no Jeff?' said Nikki, greatly daring.

'That's enough of that!' snapped Kate, whacking Nikki back into line without effort.

After supper Toby did a little careful probing of his own. Nikki was on the phone to one of her friends, and he was helping his mum with the washing up.

'Mum, about Jeff, and the doc, and everything . . .'

'Yes?' She wasn't too cordial, but she didn't snap his head off, so he decided to carry on.

'Well, we like the doc a lot, and he likes us.'

'Yes.' Her tone was definitely softer.

'And he likes you a lot. More than just a lot.'

A sharp sigh. 'Yes, I know. I like him, too.'

'Mum, he told me what the problem was. He said you didn't want us to know, because we might put the wrong kind of pressure on you. But I wanted you to know I'm praying about it, too.'

'Oh, Toby!' Now she was back to being sharp, slamming pans away into the cupboard. She weighed the last pan in her hand, not really seeing it. 'I just don't know . . . I'm so confused . . . not that it's any business of yours to be praying for me, Toby Webb!'

'If I believe in it, I don't see why not!'

She was still holding the pan, so maybe it was all right to go on. 'Mum, you don't not believe, do you?'

'It's hard to explain, Toby. You think when you're grown up that everything's going to be clear cut. That you'll know what you want. Or at least, which road to choose. But you see, Toby, I've been down this road before, with your father. I thought I was getting close to understanding about Jesus, but when your father died, it was such a shock, so terrible . . . it took me years to . . . you never really get over it. I couldn't see any of the love of Jesus surrounding me then. I put it all out of my mind. But now . . . I just don't know!'

'But couldn't we just move into the doc's flat, where we'd be safe? Just till you did feel sure?'

'No, I couldn't do that to him. It wouldn't be fair, knowing how he feels about me . . . about all of us.'

'Well, I'm going to go on praying and . . .'

'Toby Webb, how you do go on and on . . . and you

haven't rinsed this pan properly. Look at the suds on it. We'll all get tummy troubles if you don't rinse it off.'

'I'll do it again. But Mum . . .'

'Let's change the subject.'

'I am. I wanted to tell you. I'm going to be a doctor when I grow up.'

She sat down, legs sprawled, and looked at him. She made as if to speak a couple of times, but didn't. He finished the washing up, and wiped round the bowl, which he didn't often do, but now was a moment not to get into any more trouble, so he did it.

She said, 'Did Gareth put you up to this?'

He couldn't make out if she were pleased or not.

'No. I thought of it all by myself. But I told him.'

'You should have told me first. Oh, you'll probably change your mind a dozen times before you grow up.'

'I don't think so. I'm going to talk to the teachers at school about it, when I go back.'

'I couldn't stand two of you working all hours.'

'Then you are thinking seriously about him!'

She looked away, her shoulders slumped. Toby thought she looked exactly like Nikki at that moment. He wanted to tell her he loved her, but didn't know how. He went to lean against her, and she put her arm about him.

He said, 'You see, Nikki and I, we can't respect Jeff. And we think he doesn't really respect you, if he doesn't even ask you to marry him.'

'Maybe,' she said in a muffled voice, her head in his shoulder.

'So you'll think about the other thing some more?'

'Perhaps.' She thrust him away, pushed her fingers through her hair and asked if he knew where she'd put her cigarettes.

Toby decided to leave it for the time being. She was the sort that went off the deep end if you nagged.

12

'Red's back!' Nikki came bumping into the flat, towing her special mates, Jan and Clare. 'Jan saw him go into the arcade this morning, and we've all just seen him cross the road to the mobile caff. I yelled to him, but he didn't hear me.'

'Gone to fetch some chips for old man Joe, or one of his mates, I expect,' said Jan. 'Me dad says he can't understand how Joe Clark gets away with it. They're pretty sure he's the one behind the break-ins, and that he hides the stuff somewhere till he can sell it outside the district. Me dad's cousin is a policeman, and he knows!'

Nikki said, 'So that's why the police keep raiding the arcade? But they haven't found anything.'

'They gotta get the right password,' said Clare. 'You say, "Open Sesame", and a secret door in the Den of Delights opens up, and there's the loot.'

'Only there is no secret door,' said Nikki, with scorn in her voice. 'It's only a lock-up shop, and there's nothing in it except the machines and the pay booth.'

'What about the caravan?' said Toby. 'Have they looked there?'

'Where's to look?' demanded Jan. 'You can see it all from the street, except into their loo.'

'Well, I'm going down to talk to Red,' said Toby. The others came, too.

Red was just coming away from the café, his arms full of packages and tins of Coke. He tried to duck out of their way, but they surrounded him.

'Where've you been?' asked Toby. 'We want to talk to you.'

'Well, I don't want to talk to you. So get out of my way . . . Shrimp!'

Something large loomed up above them. It folded its tattooed arms, and glared down at the twins.

'Are you messing about with Red?' It was big Baldy, making it clear that he was on Red's side. Toby and the girls silently made way for Red to cross the road and disappear into the arcade.

'Scarper!' barked Baldy. They scarpered. Fats was just coming down the road, and Skinny was just coming up, so they all met on the corner.

'Red's back, but he's not talking,' reported Nikki, 'and he's got some powerful protection.'

'He called me "Shrimp," ' said Toby. 'Just like Old Man Joe.'

'Don't give it no mind,' said Fats. 'You'll shoot up one of these days, you'll see.'

'The thing is,' said Toby, trying not to care about his lack of height, 'do we abandon Red to his fate, or do we try to do something about it?'

'Aren't we being a bit melodramatic?' enquired Clare.

'No!' said Skinny and Fats together.

'So . . . Council of War up in my room?' said Toby.

They adjourned to Toby's bedroom, where they could see the Den and the building site, and the church tower, and peer over the sill to watch the comings and goings at the café below.

'Order!' cried Nikki, rapping on the bedside table with Toby's ruler. 'What's first on the agenda? And don't anyone try to be funny and say "minutes of the last meeting".'

'Getting Red out of Joe's clutches?'

'Getting rid of the arcade.' That was Fats.

'How can we?' Skinny put in his word.

'The Den's packed out,' reported Toby, from his position by the window. 'Lots of kids from school, kids we know.'

Jan said, 'Two kids from our landing in the flats have been grounded for nicking money from their mums' purses, to play in the Den . . .'

'We know there's worse things happened than that, said Fats.

'No, we don't *know*,' said Toby, 'any more than the police *know*. We all suspect, but without evidence, how can we get anywhere?'

'We know – oh, all right, we suspect – that Joe and his mum are egging kids on to steal for them, and are fencing the goods . . . somehow.'

'Nikki,' said Toby. 'Did Joe ever ask you to steal for him?'

'No, never.'

'You gotta be more in debt than Nikki was,' said Skinny in a small voice. 'You gotta be pretty desperate. At least, that's what I heard.'

'Where did you hear it?'

Skinny wriggled a bit, and then said, 'Well, Red mighta hinted, sort of. Only, I din't unnerstand at the time.'

Toby sighed. 'Which means it probably was Red that I saw, on the day we were burgled.'

'It makes me feel sick,' said Nikki, with some violence. 'When I think he was our friend, and he knew I loved that little locket . . . and there was our telly, and mum's portable . . .'

Skinny said, glancing at Fats' considerable bulk, 'Could someone pay Red a visit on the quiet-like, and "talk" to him?'

'That's not the way,' protested Fats.

'Red was our friend,' said Toby. 'I was stupid enough to get involved in playing the machines myself, I know it changed me. I couldn't stop thinking about it. I suppose that's how gamblers feel. I even stopped praying. I'm out of it now, but I can understand how it affects people.'

'I liked it at first,' said Jan. 'I thought I could take it or leave it. Only then I din't have enough for swimming this week, and had to borrow off Clare, and she was real snirky about it.'

'Too right I was,' said Clare, giving Jan a friendly punch.

'So what do we do?' asked Nikki. 'Give up? Red will end up in a special school if we don't do something, and lots more people will lose their tellies and their silver lockets.'

'We pray, for a start,' said Toby.

'What's the good of praying?' said Nikki, kneeling on the windowsill and looking out. 'What we want is action. We've got to clear them out of the place, somehow. Look, there's millions of them. They crowd into the Den, come over to the caff for chips, and then back to the Den. They've taken the place over.'

'Joe Clark must be making a mint,' said Skinny, 'and his mum. They're even charging for their loo.'

'The Den hasn't got a loo,' said Nikki.

'No, the caff. At the back, down the passage.'

'The caff's got a loo inside the caravan,' said Jan. 'You can see it, from outside. A little one, in the corner at the back.'

'I didn't mean the loo inside the caravan,' said Skinny. 'That's for Ma and her helpers. I meant the one they've got for special customers, that you get to through the passage under the wall here. She lets people use it, but she charges. She wouldn't let me, 'cos I'd only got 5p.

She says it's 10p, and I hadn't got it.'

'I think we should pray about it,' said Toby. 'All of us.'

'What, here and now?' said Nikki, who considered prayer the last resort, only to be indulged in when no-one could see her.

'Yes,' said Fats, 'that would be best. Toby, you've got the gift of putting things straight. Will you be our spokesman?'

Toby shut his eyes, and tried to concentrate.

'Dear Jesus, you know what's happening around here. How everything's going wrong for our friend, Red. We know the machines aren't evil in themselves, but have encouraged the evil in us. Help us to keep straight. And about Red, will you please show us what to do and how to do it?'

He was silent, but no-one spoke. He opened his eyes, and saw they'd all got their eyes closed, even those lolling across his bed and sprawled on the floor. Toby closed his eyes again.

Dear Jesus. He didn't speak aloud this time. There's so much evil around. Maybe it's because of the church being under wraps. It's almost as if the doc's moving out has made room for evil men to move in. Or am I going bananas? We do need help, please.

Someone shifted their legs, and someone else sighed. Toby opened his eyes and smiled at Fats, who smiled back. Most of them were smiling, now.

'Ooh, I'm stiff,' groaned Jan, stretching.

A sudden loud bang from the building site made them all jump. Dust drifted through the window, which was open at the bottom. The dust made Toby cough, so he leaned forward to shut the window.

'There's a funny thing,' he said. 'There's a boy from our school leaving the outside loo, now.'

'What's funny about that?'

'I saw him go in when we started the meeting. He had two large plastic bags with him then. Heavy ones. He hasn't got them now.'

'Musta forgot them. Left them in the loo.'

'Come on! They were big. How could you forget two really big bags like that?'

Fats said, 'I expect he was fetching groceries for Joe's mum.'

'Nah,' said Skinny. 'She gets them delivered. Big Joe goes to the market for her in his van, two or three times a week. Early. And he takes her rubbish away to the dump, too. Late at night, when he's closed up the Den for the evening.'

'Suppose,' said Toby, 'that it is she who's looking after the stolen goods, not him. Suppose Joe brings them to her in his van, disguised as food for the caff, and takes them away later, pretending they're rubbish for the dump.'

'No room to keep anything in the caravan,' said Fats.

'Well, in the passageway between the caravan and the wall.'

'That's their outside loo. Besides, don't you think the police have looked? And there isn't enough room, anyway, not for tellies and stereos and videos and all sorts.'

Toby said, 'OK, but I'm sure there's something going on there. Suppose we keep watch on who goes in and out?'

'Watch the loos? Give over!'

'Well, you got a better idea?'

No one had a better idea, though no-one liked it much. But, it was the holidays, it had come on to rain again, and they hadn't enough money to go to the cinema. So they decided to take turns to play Monopoly on the floor, and whoever wasn't playing should keep watch out of the window.

By the end of the afternoon it was clear they *were* on to something, though they were not sure what. Quite a few people spoke to Mrs Clark and then went down the passageway to the outside loo. They stayed there for varying amounts of time, but none were there for less than ten minutes, and some for much longer.

'It's an odd sort of loo that can keep them occupied for so long,' said Toby.

'A mystery loo,' said Jan, giggling. 'A magic loo.'

'I think I'd like a look at this strange loo,' said Toby. 'Maybe tonight, after the caff and the Den have shut down for the night, and there's no-one about. Maybe they've got a trunk hidden down there, or some other cache for the stolen goods.'

'Now wait a minute,' said Fats. 'This lot doesn't go in for Sunday School treats. This lot plays rough. I think we'll get Brains and Tooley, my football mates, in on this. I'll go round to see them tonight, and tomorrow we'll set the trap!'

Toby knew that what Fats had said was sensible. The Clarks were not people you could cross and get away with it. Toby had no intention of doing anything that night . . . until he saw the duck.

It wasn't big. Perhaps big enough to cover a postage stamp. It was one of the ducks which Jeff had given Nikki, and which she'd carelessly stuck all over the place.

At least, it looked like the same kind of duck. It might not be one of Nikki's ducks, of course, but Toby had never seen any others in the neighbourhood, and Nikki had been so disgusted with Jeff's present that she'd got rid of them straight away.

She'd stuck some on the telly, and some on her school bag, and one on the cardboard trinket box in which she'd kept her bits and pieces of jewellery. Including the silver locket.

And there was the box, spilling out of a black plastic bag of rubbish, dumped in the door of the old surgery. The box was a bit squashed as if someone had trodden on it, but the duck was unmistakably still a duck.

Toby picked the box up, but it was empty. No locket, no nothing. So how had it got there? And where had it been, all this time?

That was when Toby decided not to wait, but to start the investigation by himself.

13

Toby tried not to get too excited. He'd found a black plastic bag, and it contained something which had been stolen from their flat. OK. The first thing was to preserve the evidence. He opened the plastic bag, and found several second-hand handbags inside, the sort that might be left over at the end of a jumble sale.

Toby did a double-take. They weren't left-overs. They were the discarded handbags from muggings. A handbag was snatched, the mugger ran off with it, ripped out anything of use to him, and threw away the handbag. Into the rubbish.

Toby looked around. What if he'd been spotted from the Den? He must get this stuff to the cop shop straight away. It wouldn't do to leave it, not even to go upstairs and make a quick phone call.

'What you done with that other bag?' Baldy's voice was menacing and so close that Toby jumped. Then he realised it had come from round the corner by the café. 'You . . . !' There was the sound of a blow. 'Don't you know no better than to leave it out there? Bring it back here, and you'd better hope no-one's spotted it!'

Toby melted into the doorway to their flat, and held his breath. Someone – he daren't look to see who – scrabbled into the doorway of the old surgery, and then there was a rustle as the plastic bag was picked up and removed. Toby was still holding the squashed cardboard box in his hand. He thought it might be missed, but apparently it wasn't. So far, so good.

He let himself through his own front door, and ran up the stairs to the kitchen, trying to be quiet. Nikki was there, listening to the radio and scowling at a comic.

Toby put the box on the table.

'Where did you get that?' screeched Nikki, grabbing for it. 'That's my . . .'

'In a plastic sack of stuff which had been dumped in the surgery doorway by mistake. I heard Baldy telling someone off for leaving it out, and sending them for it, so I hid, and then came up here to tell you. I couldn't be absolutely sure it was your box.'

'Well, it is. Which proves that . . .'

'Tell Fats, will you? I'm going back downstairs. I'll watch from across the road, see if they load sacks into Old Joe's van . . .'

'Right! I'll phone around and see who I can get, and then we can tell Mum . . .'

Toby shot back down the stairs. Business seemed to be going on as usual over the road at the Den, and at the café, too. He peeped round the corner into the Wasteland. The security lights had just been switched on, and the dog was roaming around, sniffing, just inside the wire fence. The ghetto blaster on the café-counter was turned right up. Mrs Clark and Baldy were serving.

There wasn't any sign of the plastic bag. Toby hesitated. Was the squashed cardboard box enough evidence for him to take to the police? It was just an old box with a duck on it. What he needed was one of those handbags which the villains had been throwing away. Now, if he could only get one of those . . .

All he had to do was go down the passage to the outside loo, find the plastic bag, and scarper with it.

No-one was taking a blind bit of notice of him. It wouldn't take a minute.

It was dark in the passageway. He closed his eyes to accustom them to the darkness, and slid along the wall. He could see the door of the loo blocking off the end of the passage.

No sack.

They must have put it back inside the loo.

There was a Yale-type lock on the door, but the door had warped and it hadn't shut properly. Toby inched it open. Nothing but darkness. He curled his hands around his eyes to see better. Then threw the door open.

There was no loo inside, only a bucket with a lid on it. The rest was space!

To Toby's left was the side of the caravan. In front of him was a sheet of corrugated iron, forming the back of the shed. Above was another sheet of corrugated iron, making the roof. To the right . . .

The wall of the old surgery should have been on the right, but it was half concealed by an old curtain, nailed into the brickwork. One side of the curtain had been looped up on a nail, and behind that was a door which had no right to be there. The door led through the wall into the building below the Webbs' flat.

The doorway had been roughly hacked out of the bricks. The door frame was a gash job, not very well finished, but its existence provided an explanation for much that had been puzzling Toby and the police. The door was well concealed from view, because it could only be approached through the outside loo, and when the curtain was hanging down, it would conceal from curious eyes the fact that the wall had been tampered with.

A light was shining around cracks in the door. Toby put out a hand to try the lock, and . . .

Heavy hands fell on his shoulders, and propelled him through the door and into the space beyond.

He fell with his feet in a tangle of plastic bags. Some-one screeched, and a man's voice said, 'What the . . . !'

'Joe saw him snooping, and sent across to say we'll have to deal with him,' Mrs Clark said.

Toby looked up into Red's scared eyes. Red had been helping Yellowtop to pack second-hand tellies and videos into cardboard boxes. They'd been working at a make-shift trestle table, stacked high with a variety of goods. Beyond was a small mountain of bags and boxes, the contents of which were being sorted by a big lad whom Toby recognised as coming from his own school.

'You can't do anything to me,' said Toby. 'I've got people watching me.'

'Like this one?' There was a squawk, and Nikki was thrust into the room by Baldy.

Baldy was grinning. 'Found her outside, following the other one. I checked but there's no-one else.'

Toby got his arm round Nikki, who was holding her wrist, with her face screwed up in pain. 'You all right?'

'Yes, but I didn't have time to let anyone . . .'

'That's just what I wanted to know,' said the woman, beaming. The wider her grin grew, the less Toby liked it. She got hold of the twins, and thrust them before her, through into the back room which had once been the doctor's, and which was now jam packed with equipment. Toby recognised two more of Nikki's ducks on their old TV.

Mrs Clark pushed them into what had once been the dispensary cupboard. There were still shelves in it, and there was only just room for them both to stand up.

'Hold on!' It was Red, his voice shaking. 'Don't put Toby in there. He'll die. He has asthma.'

'You mind your own bizzy,' said the woman, giving Red a backhanded clout. 'If he gets sick then it's his own fault for poking his nose in where he ought not to be.'

She slammed the door on the twins, and locked it. The last thing Toby saw before the blackness enclosed them, was Red's frightened face. Then all he could hear was his own hurried breathing, and Nikki's.

'You all right?' she whispered. 'I lied to her. I did phone Fats. He was out so I left a message. He'll come and get us soon.'

'Who did you leave the message with? One of his young brothers?'

Nikki was silent, which meant she had. Oh well, thought Toby. No doubt the woman will let us out soon. She's put us in here as a punishment, but the darkness won't frighten us, because we're in it together.

His breathing wasn't good, though.

'Toby!' whispered Nikki. 'There's no air in here! Do you remember the doc saying he'd been to a lot of trouble to get this cupboard really well made, because he kept all his drugs in it? We're going to die of suffocation!'

'Don't panic. Don't talk. Don't do anything. We've got to conserve air. Let's sit down and think how to get out . . .'

'But don't you see?' This is what Red was so frightened of? Being shut in the cupboard! She probably doesn't realise that two of us will use up air so much more quickly! We're going to die!'

'No, we're not. Just keep quiet. Think. Pray if you can.'

He knew she usually did get round to praying when she was up against it. They squatted on the floor. Toby felt all around the edges of the door, but it did seem to be air-tight. The walls had been plastered and kept in good condition till the doc left. Ironic, to die in the doc's old surgery.

Toby felt his mind clouding over. He was praying in snatches. Lord, help us . . . help everyone who they've hurt . . . help poor Red . . . and that other lad . . . please, help Nikki to keep calm and talk to you . . . we're in such danger, but you know all about danger . . .

if we have to die . . . poor Mum . . . help her in her search . . . don't let this turn her away from Jesus . . .

He drifted off into a darkness which had become comforting rather than a menace . . .

Light broke in on them, and a babel of sound. People were shouting, trying to help him to stand.

Toby shook his head, trying to remember where he was and what he was doing in such a dark, cramped place.

'Carry him out!'

Toby was scooped up and carried out into the open air. The first thing he recognised was the face of Fats. Brains and Tooley were hovering over Nikki, and she was fast regaining the use of her tongue. Toby could hear her babbling away.

Tony said, 'So your brother got the message to you in time!'

'No,' said Fats, grinning, 'Red phoned me from the call box at the end of the road. He phoned the police, too. It's all over bar the shouting.'

And so it was. By the weekend, when the doc took the Webbs on their long-planned outing, Toby had even stopped using his inhaler. The four of them had a really good time at the Easter Fair and then went back to the doc's for an informal supper. The meal consisted of lots of things the doc had bought in the delicatessen, and some that he'd forgotten he had in the fridge.

The party was in a bubbly mood, because so many good things had been happening since the power of the gang had been broken. The police thought it unlikely that Red would have to go 'away' but very likely that the rest of them would, and for a long time, too. The Webbs would even get their TV back soon, though the rest of their things seemed to have been sold and might never be recovered.

The church was steadily rising from the ground and you could see it was going to be just what they needed. Another marvellous thing had happened: the developers had decided that in the present economic climate they couldn't afford to pull down Paradise Row and rebuild. The houses were going to be gutted and modernised. So although the Webbs would have to move out while the alterations took place, they could move back later on, if they wished. In the meantime the council had promised them the next big flat that came up.

'So sucks to Jeff,' said Nikki, and wasn't even checked for rudeness.

The doc was in great form, laughing and joking as they cleared the table. Kate was in a strangely quiet mood, though she didn't appear to be unhappy.

'Twins,' she said, 'why don't you go upstairs and have a look round the flat?'

'We've been,' said Nikki. 'Don't you remember, we went round before tea, while you were getting it ready.'

'Oh, yes, of course,' said Kate, going pink.

'If you mean you want to be alone with the doc, then just say so,' said Nikki.

Now it was the doc's turn to go red. 'Er, well, why not? Why don't you two explore my part of the house, especially the attics. You can find your way, can't you?'

Nikki beat Toby to the door by a short head.

'Bet you he's making her an offer she can't refuse!' said Nikki, as they pounded up the stairs.

Toby grinned. He'd missed his Bible a couple of nights previously, and found it by his mum's bed. He hadn't said anything to her, and she hadn't said anything to him, but it looked as if the doc knew what was going on all right.

Most of the first floor doors had been locked because they were part of the self-contained flat which the doc let. Toby knew what those rooms looked like. They'd make a good place to live in; but even better if they were opened up and rejoined the rest of the house.

Toby found the narrower stairs leading to the attics first, but Nikki pushed past him, screaming with delight. Toby followed her, more slowly. He had a suffocating feeling in his chest, but it wasn't fear. It was an immense and pleasurable excitement.

'Wow!' said Nikki, entering a room with an electric train set laid out on the floor. Nikki had always been more interested in trains than in dolls. 'Do you think he'll let me use this?'

Toby went through into the wide back attic, which had dormer windows on two sides. One window faced south, and the other faced over the London skyline towards St. Paul's and the City.

'What you got?' yelled Nikki.

'Wow, look at all those church spires!' said Toby. 'It's something else! There's too many to count.'

Nikki followed him in. 'Can you see our church?'

'Yes, but many, many more.'

Toby thought, God really is everywhere. I knew it in my head before, but I didn't know it in my heart. I only saw the one building before, but now . . . I'm just beginning to understand . . .

The doc and Kate came into the room, holding hands. The evening sun shone on their faces, and they were both smiling.

Kate said, 'Well, kids. You seem to have made yourselves at home here.'

'Can I have a go with the trains?' said Nikki.

Toby looked at the doc, and then at his mum, and he realised it wasn't the evening light on their faces, but happiness. Toby saw that his mum had accepted Jesus into her heart, and the doc's offer, and that they were going to be married. And this would be his room, and maybe he'd have to go away to school, if that was what the doc thought was for the best. But it didn't matter, he could stand it, because there were churches everywhere, and God was everywhere, and that was, as Fats would have said, the bottom line.